Highland Wolf Clan
Despair and Destiny
Book 4

By

A K Michaels

Dedication

I would like to dedicate this to someone that has agreed to allow some pictures to be used as the backdrop of this cover. Her name is Shelly and yes I named a character after her! Shelly's taken some stunning photos of the area at her gorgeous home in Deming and graciously allowed my girls to use them.

Thank you, Shelly, I really appreciate it hon. Hope you enjoy the book and especially the next one which is focused on your character!

~ Chapter 1 ~

Fergie was torn from sleep by loud banging noises on the back door. The hammering so strong that he was sure the cabin actually shook. His sleep addled brain slowly coming awake as his arm automatically reached for his mate and finding nothing but empty space. His stomach lurched when he realized Angel was not beside him and he shook his head to clear it of the last vestiges of slumber as he tried to engage his brain.

The next sound he heard almost stopped his heart; Angel's gasp of fear and her voice pleading, "Stop, please, stop."

He didn't even think, moving with lightning speed, entering the kitchen to see a huge hulk hovering over his mate. As large hands held her shoulders, shaking her and shouting down at her terrified face. "Where is she? Where the fuck is she?"

Fergie growled, his beast eager to make an appearance and take on this threat, his anger so great he didn't even recognize the male holding Angel. "Get your fucking hands off my mate or I'll rip your fucking throat out!"

Two sets of astonished eyes landed on him, Angel's hand flying to her mouth as she exclaimed. "It worked! Thank the Goddess, it worked."

Jacob's mouth fell open, his face a mask of amazement as Fergie stomped toward them. "I said, take your hands off my mate, Jacob, or I *will* take you down!"

"What the hell?" Jacob cursed, looking at Fergie as if he were seeing imaginary things.

Angel pulled away, rushing to Fergie and falling into his outstretched arms. "It worked, mon loupe. It worked."

Fergie's heart slowed as he became aware that Angel was no longer in danger, but only for a mere moment before he realized he was on his own feet in the kitchen. Looking down at Angel with a frown then staring at his legs as if they weren't his. "What the fuck's going on?" he gasped as Angel started to sob.

"Please forgive me, my love," Angel pleaded, her fingers digging into his chest. "I didn't know what else to do. You were so stubborn and I'm sorry. Please don't hate me."

"What did you do?" Fergie asked, his amazement at being on his own legs again still rushing through him.

"Rebecca came while you were sleeping and healed you, she . . ."

Fergie cut her off. "What? You did what? Why would you *do* that?"

Angel's sobs worsened as her red eyes glistened up at him. "Because I *love* you! That's

2

why! You wouldn't let anyone help heal you and I'm your mate. I couldn't stand by and not do anything when I knew there *was* something that could be done. You're my everything, Fergie, and you were dying inside, right in front of my eyes."

Jacob's voice boomed out, interrupting them. "I don't give a fuck about your little domestic squabble. Becca is gone, she's missing! I tracked her scent here and I found *this* outside on the ground."

He held up Rebecca's phone, now dirty and covered in bits of leaves. "She never goes anywhere without her phone and she damn sure didn't just go for a jaunt in the forest. So, Angel, why don't you tell me where my fucking mate is?"

Fergie pulled her tighter within his arms, snarling at Jacob. "Watch your tone, Jacob!"

Angel shook her head frantically. "I don't know where she is. I promise I don't. She came, healed Fergie then left. I've not seen her since and that must've been about five hours ago. I'm so sorry, Jacob. I don't know what's happened to her."

Jacob's head fell back, a deafening roar erupting from him as he fought to control himself. Fergie looked at Angel then the distraught Jacob, his heritage flaring to life as he became Alpha. "Angel, we'll discuss what you did later, in private. However, it looks as if something's happened to Rebecca so we need to help Jacob to find his mate. First, Jacob, are you certain you can't scent her leaving the area behind the cabin? Possibly wandering off in the dark and getting lost? Second, Angel, put some clothes on and get up to Cam and let him know we have a problem."

Angel darted away as Jacob paced back and forth, anger, fear and despair rolling off him in great waves. His eyes, when he turned to Fergie, were haunted. "Fergie, where is she? I tracked her here, then she left, got only a few feet and then nothing. It's as if she simply disappeared into thin air and her phone fell from the sky. *Fuck!*"

Fergie walked over, grabbing hold of Jacob's shoulder, his tone firm and hard. "Stop! You won't help her if you don't focus, Jacob. Rein in your fear and concentrate your terror into finding her. Now, wait here while I go and get dressed and while I'm doing that try and think on what might've happened. If she has any enemies she's spoken to you about then that would be a good place to start. Okay?"

Jacob nodded, his eyes almost pleading to tell him this was all a misunderstanding. Fergie tightened his grip on the large Wolf. "I understand, Jacob. I do. But you need to get a grip on yourself. I'll only be a moment, just hang in there and try to think of anything that will help us find her."

Angel rushed back in, now dressed and tears still in her eyes. "I'll go and get Cam."

"Be quick," Fergie ordered. "The sooner we get started the faster we'll find her."

"Okay," Angel whispered, turning to run out of the cabin.

Fergie strode away, only now able to concentrate on what he was doing; walking on his own two legs. His heart sped up, happiness and joy rushing through him at the same time as upset and anger at Angel's deception. Never in a million years would he have thought she was capable of deceiving him. However, that was a conversation for another time, once they helped Jacob. Now his only thought was on what might've happened to the sassy Witch.

Fergie liked Rebecca, he loved her quick comebacks, her wit, and her downright rebellious streak. In fact, she reminded him of himself in many ways and prayed they found her quickly. He dreaded to think what Jacob would do if they didn't.

Once in his room, he tore off his underwear and pulled out clean clothes, finding it strange reaching for things from such a height. Normally he would be several feet lower, in his chair which was still sitting beside the bed. A snarl escaped him as he looked at the chair he'd considered a prison. Holding him back from helping his Pack when they needed him the most, and from protecting his father from Phillipe Dupont and his men.

Slamming the drawer so hard the dresser shook, Fergie placed his hands on top, leaning forward and breathing deeply. What had he done? His eagerness not to upset his father may well have been the thing that caused his death. If he'd reached out to Cam earlier and asked for help, then maybe he wouldn't have spent months locked in the chair and he'd maybe, just possibly, been able to avert the death of the person he idolized. He shook his head knowing that his train of thought would not help locate Rebecca and that was his priority right now.

Moving around the room quickly, he dressed but left his boots untied and his jeans loose at his waist. He envisaged going Wolf real soon to track the missing Witch and his beast howled in glee at being able to run free once more. The last few months he'd rarely transformed, his shame at not being able to move stopping him and the only person that'd seen him in Wolf form had been Angel, in the privacy of their home.

Now he could run with the Pack again. Although worried for Rebecca, he couldn't tamp down his enthusiasm at the prospect of running free once more. As he passed by the mirror, he saw himself grinning like an idiot and he stopped, taking in his tall, muscular frame, surprised that his legs didn't even appear weak. Whatever the Witch had done she'd done it well because he'd never felt better, stronger, more capable than he did right now.

Wiping the smile from his face he left their room, a fleeting thought of what he'd do to Angel the first time they were alone. She'd only ever had sex with him while he wasn't fully functioning, now she'd truly see what he was capable of.

His long legs striding purposefully along the hallway to find Jacob still pacing in the kitchen. The distraught look on his face pulling at Fergie's heart. "We'll find her, Jacob."

The large PI turned sharply. "Will we? I have no fucking clue what's going on, so how do we do that?"

"First of all, you need to calm down." Fergie's head fell to the side, staring intently at the other Wolf. "You *will* have some information, it's just that you're too emotional at the moment to think clearly. So, why don't you try and think back on anything that Rebecca has said that would make you stop and think 'that's wrong.'"

Jacob snarled, his lips baring his teeth as he placed his hands on the counter. Fergie stayed silent, letting the man ponder on his mate and hoping Jacob could think of a lead. Before Jacob could come up with anything, the front door banged open, Cam, Jinx, Mac, and Rory rushing in.

"What the hell is going on?" Cam spat out, his eyes widening when he saw Fergie on his feet.

"Rebecca's missing." Fergie shrugged. "She apparently came here late last night to heal me and then she didn't make it back to Jacob. He found her phone outside in the dirt and he says her trail just ended."

"I see." Cam frowned. "Jacob, how are you

holding up?"

Jacob snarled again. "I'm not." He spat out, shaking his head furiously.

"I understand." Cam came over, patting Jacob's arm. "Can you think of anyone that would want to do her harm? Or anything that's happened that's unusual, or off? Anything at all, Jacob."

"I can't think, Cam." Jacob looked panic-stricken. "I don't mean I can't think of anything, I mean I *can't* think. My brain isn't functioning."

Jinx stepped forward. "I may have something."

All eyes turned to the Beta, as Fergie spoke. "What? What you got, Jinx?"

"I was talking to Rebecca and she, well, she was saying she was a bit worried about her—" Jinx stopped, frowning. "Shit, what was it she called her? Jacob, what's the word for her Beta?"

Jacob stood up straighter, his eyes coming alive. "Maiden."

"Yes, that's it." Jinx nodded. "She was saying there was something going on with her maiden. She wasn't replying to her texts or calls and she wasn't happy that Rebecca wasn't pairing with a Witch. At the time I felt uneasy and hoped it'd sort itself out. Jacob, do you know if it did? Did Rebecca get hold of this girl?"

"No," Jacob shook his head, his tone furious. "Bridget's her name and she was definitely unhappy

8

about me being a Wolf. I know Becca tried to contact her just yesterday, but, again, the little bitch didn't respond."

"Good." Cam walked towards the back door. "That's a place to start. Jacob, show me where you found her phone. Jinx, you get Stracey to get everything she can on this Bridget person and also get her to contact the High Priest. Afraid I've forgotten his name, but he should be able to help, hopefully."

"On it." Jinx turned and ran from the cabin.

Cam opened the door and went outside, Jacob on his heels. "Over there." Jacob pointed, only a couple of yards from the back door.

"Give me some room." Cam held his arms out, stopping any of the others from going in front of him. "I'm going to see if I can sense what happened."

As Cam stood still, his face a mask of concentration, Jacob stayed right behind him, Fergie next to him and the other's crowding the doorway. Only a moment later Cam's head swiveled off to the right. "Magic. The place is steeped in magic but I can smell something, it's weird, but it's . . . hold on." Cam scowled, his eyes closed tight. "Drugs. She's been drugged. Jacob, can't you scent that?"

Jacob stepped forward, his own eyes closing as he took a deep breath in, using his Wolf abilities to smell whatever it was that Cam had. It hit him smack bang in the face and he shook his head, a rumble of anger erupting from his throat. "Fuck! I do know that smell, Cam. I've smelled it before when doing some private PI work. Remember that kidnapping case I worked a couple of years back? Well, this is the same stuff they used on that kid to keep him knocked out. Some fucker has knocked her out to stop her using her magic."

"Yeah, that was my first thought too." Cam agreed. "An angry Rebecca would soon take someone down that was trying to abduct her. I guess they thought this was the only way to do it without getting their asses kicked."

"I'll rip them apart!" Jacob shouted, his voice loud in the pre-dawn light. "Whoever's done this is gonna see just what a fucking angry Wolf can do."

"I can see their trail." Cam pointed off to the right. "It's similar to the one I saw when Dupont used that Warlock to hide them being on our land. It's a Witch, Jacob, at least one, possibly two. We can follow the trail but I suspect they had a vehicle nearby and as she's been gone for hours, that means they could be anywhere."

Jacob grabbed Cam's shoulder, shaking it hard. "We need to try, Cam. We have to follow the trail and see where it leads. If there are vehicle tracks then that's my expertise. I'll be able to find out what vehicle was used and that should narrow down the

10

suspect list." Jacob let go of Cam, striding away for a few yards before stopping and turning back. "They did this 'cause I'm a Wolf, not a Witch. Why didn't I know I could be putting her in danger? I should've known."

Fergie shook his head. "No, you couldn't. How were you to know that someone would take it this far? You couldn't have known, Jacob, but regardless of that, you need to concentrate on getting her back. Not on what ifs."

"Fergie's right." Cam started to undress. "Jacob, Fergie, come with me, Mac and Rory, can you liaise with Jinx and Stracey and have any information ready for our return?"

"Sure." Mac nodded, disappearing back inside the cabin.

"Fergie, are you okay to come with us?" Cam asked, his eyebrow raised in query.

"I think so." Fergie shrugged. "Won't know 'til I try but I feel better than I've ever felt. Whatever the hell Rebecca did, it's worked, and I feel strong and more than capable."

"Okay, if you're sure." Cam folded his clothes and put them on the back steps of the cabin. "Can you protect our rear? We don't know what's going on, or if there's any threat still around, and I don't want anything attacking us from behind."

"Yes," Fergie said, his beast growling inside his head at the thought of whoever had taken the

Witch still being on their land. His clothes quickly joined Cam's, Jacob's falling beside them a moment later.

Cam's transformation was quick, as usual, Fergie watching as the large midnight black Wolf appeared before him. He didn't look at Jacob, focusing on his own change intently. His beast so eager that his own morphing was quicker than normal, taking his breath away as his reddish brown Wolf appeared and letting out a long, pent-up howl of glee.

His beast pranced about, his nose picking up all the scents of the forest and then its snout wrinkled in distaste at the smell of magic pervading the air. Fergie's relief at once more being able to move around in his Wolf form was overshadowed by the reason for it being present now.

Jacob's immense Wolf shook before him, its fur quivering as its snout lowered to the last place his mate stood. A low keening sound rumbling from its throat as a massive paw clawed at the ground. Cam's Wolf moved closer, nudging Jacob's before turning around and loping off into the forest.

Fergie waited until Jacob had followed and then he trailed behind, alert for any danger.

~ Chapter 2 ~

Cam clearly saw the trail of magic, a light blue mist floating just above the ground. He learned early in life that each Witch's magic left a different trail, color, scent, but this one felt "off" in a way he wasn't quite grasping. Yet. He'd get to the bottom of it and find this person, and Rebecca, no matter what it took.

He could feel Jacob's Wolf at his heels, the track they were on too narrow for their beasts to be side by side. A time or two his friend's impatience causing his Wolf to nudge him along, obviously desperate to see if it would lead them to Rebecca. Cam knew different. Nobody with an ounce of sense would still be on Pack land and holding a Wolf's mate hostage.

That would be just plain suicide.

The trail was easy to follow so Cam's mind wandered to the shock of Fergie being on his feet. To say he was happy for his cousin was a huge understatement, he was ecstatic to the extreme. However, he also spotted Fergie's true nature shining through—that of Alpha. What a conundrum.

Cam never wanted to be Alpha. Fought against it his entire life, but now that he was, he didn't think he could walk away. Could he?

This wasn't the time to be thinking about that. They needed to find Rebecca, as soon as possible. Shaking his large Wolf's head to clear his thoughts, he concentrated on the trail. He tried to pick up anything else that would help locate her and soon he realized that there were two people involved. The trail was narrow, so to carry Rebecca the kidnapper would have either had to be very strong, which he doubted going by the impressions in the ground. Or, there were two.

Cam stopped, his snout lowering to the ground to take in everything that he could. Rebecca's scent was clear in the air, her perfume one that he knew well. However, there were two other distinct smells. One a light, flowery perfume, and the other a darker, musky aftershave. A man and a woman were involved.

Now all they had to do was find out who and then find where they'd taken his friend.

Jacob's anxious yipping urged them on. Cam picking up speed and now tearing through the forest with Jacob and Fergie behind him. It wasn't long until they came to a clearing which had a rough track leading to it. Cam saw the impression of wheels in the grass; this was where they'd parked and where they'd brought Rebecca.

Cam morphed quickly, stalking around and taking in every minute detail. "They parked here and there's a man and a woman involved."

"I know." Jacob replied, causing Cam to spin around. He hadn't realized his friend had changed too.

Jacob pointed to the track. "They went that way and there's some soft dirt there with tire tracks. I'm going to go back and get something to take a picture of them. I can then use a program I have on my computer to find out make and model."

Cam nodded. "Okay. I won't ask where you got that 'cause I'm pretty sure you shouldn't have your hands on that technology."

Shrugging, Jacob turned away, transforming quickly and racing back the way they'd come. Cam continued to check out the area, spotting something lying hidden in the undergrowth. Rushing over and bending down Cam plucked the item up, his throat constricting when he saw a woman's velvet slipper in his hand. Even before he smelled it, he knew he'd find his friend's scent on it.

Yes. It reeked of Rebecca and Cam's heart lurched knowing she was in danger. This was proof positive that she had not left of her own volition.

"I'll find you," he whispered to himself softly.

Fergie's low growl reminding him he wasn't alone, Cam turned around. "I'm going to need your help, cousin. We all need to work together to find her."

The reddish fur on Fergie's beast ruffled as it moved its large head in a nodding motion, agreeing with Cam. "Thank you. Now we need to get back and see if Stracey and the rest have found anything out. Come on."

Cam started to run, changing mid-stride, one moment a pair of feet slapped on the ground, and the next four large paws tore along at break-neck speed. He didn't let up, going all out, back towards Camp, Fergie on his heels every step of the way. He could feel the power and strength inside his cousin's beast and knew he'd want him at his side for any trouble that lay ahead. For now, all he wanted to do was get home and see if Stracey had worked her own form of magic and found out about this Bridget person.

They were almost back at the Camp when Jacob's Wolf came running back towards them, a bag held in his jaws. Cam and Fergie got out of his way before he could knock them over, and Jacob didn't even slow down, tearing along at a speed few Wolves could match.

Once he was past, Cam and Fergie resumed their run and were soon stopping outside Fergie's cabin. Transforming quickly, they grabbed their clothes and pulled them on before going inside. Nobody was there, Cam looked to Fergie then shrugged. "Must be at the Alpha cabin. Let's go see if they've got anything we can work with."

"We'll get her, Cam." Fergie patted Cam's arm as he walked past, opening the door for them. "I know she's your friend, but we will find her."

"I know." Cam nodded. "I'll make damn sure

of it. The people responsible have no idea of the pain and suffering they're going to endure when we do catch up with them."

"Let's go." Fergie ushered him out. "I guess I'm gonna surprise a few folks today. What with me not being in my wheelchair 'n all."

Cam managed a smile. "Yes. I can't wait to see Marie. She's going to freak out, cousin."

"Yes," Fergie grinned. "She's going to go nuts."

"Fergie—" Cam stopped on the doorstep. "I also know we need to discuss things. You being healed changes things. I know that. But now isn't the time. We need to find Rebecca before Jacob goes crazy."

Fergie nodded, his head leaned to the side staring at Cam. "Yes, I understand, Cam, and no matter what comes, I need to tell you how much I appreciate all that you've done for the Pack. Or, I should say Packs, plural. It's not only this one you've helped, but I realize we need to find Rebecca. Damn, I have to thank her for what she's done, even if it's opened a can of worms."

Cam grabbed Fergie by the shoulder, giving it a squeeze. "I'm so happy that you're back on your feet. All the other stuff can be worked through later. Now, let's go and see if we have anything to work with."

"Sounds like a plan." Fergie strode quickly

away, the Camp empty as it was still early, but he knew everyone would soon know he was whole again and that brought a heap of problems. For him and the Pack.

Giving himself a shake, he carried on, his legs strong as they carried him through the Camp, towards the Alpha cabin. *His* cabin.

Cam started to jog and Fergie joined him, their speed increasing until they leaped up the stairs and onto the porch, rushing inside. The living room was pretty crowded, Mac, Rory and Jinx were there, as well as Angel, Marie and Chastity.

Marie turned, her eyes wide and immediately filling with tears. "She told me. Angel told me, but I didn't dare believe her. Oh! Fergie, you're healed. My son, you're healed."

Fergie strode over, grinning. "Yes, Mom, I'm healed and before you ask, I'm fine. There's no need for tears, Mom. Come on, stop crying, you know I hate seeing anyone crying."

Wiping her eyes with the edge of her apron, Marie reached up and kissed Fergie's cheek. "I'm so happy for you, Son."

"I know, Mom." Fergie patted her back. "But right now we have to find out what's happened to Rebecca. There'll be plenty of time to talk after we've found her. Okay?"

"Of course." Marie turned away. "I'll have some food and coffee ready shortly. You'll all need to eat before you go anywhere."

Cam could feel the happiness pouring from his aunt as she rushed back to the kitchen and he knew her mind would be in turmoil about Fergie's future within the Pack. Pushing those thoughts aside he went over to Stracey who was sitting curled up on a chair, laptop on her knees and typing furiously. "Anything?" he asked, hoping she'd found something for them to use.

Stracey nodded. "Give me one more second." She continued typing, her fingers flying over the keyboard for another moment or two before she stopped. "Okay, Bridget Mahoney, aka Rebecca's maiden. She lives in a beach house on a prime site outside LA. It's technically her parents' house, but they appear to be very affluent and more often than not are jetting all over the place. That's if they're not away on daddy's yacht. She's twenty-five, and was rather average in her studies, only just passing some subjects and failing a couple of others. Bridget hasn't worked a day in her life but she is interested in magic and has been a practicing Witch for a few years. I have her home and mobile numbers here, please don't ask how I got those, and her address. I also have Elijah's details, he's the High Priest, and hopefully he may be able to help us."

"That's great, Stracey." Cam smirked, knowing how useful his assistant was at obtaining details on just about anyone. "I think you should call

Bridget and I'll call the Priest, what's his name again?"

"Elijah." Stracey grabbed her mobile from down the side of the chair she was sitting on. "He's really nice. Quite a bit older than Rebecca, but they work well for the coven. I've met him a few times, but you know I kinda stay away from all that stuff so I don't know him overly well. However, Rebecca speaks highly of him and if she does that, then it means he's a good man."

"Okay, what's his number?" Cam already had his phone in his hand, fingers ready to dial.

Stracey passed him a note. "Here, way ahead of you." She smirked as he took the paper, walking away.

Cam heard the ringing in his ear before he sat down at the table. Marie throwing him furtive looks as she continued with preparing a mountain of food. After what appeared to be a long time Cam finally heard a soft, "Hello?"

"Hi, is this Elijah?" Cam shifted in his seat, hoping this man could help. "This is Cameron Sinclair, a friend of Rebecca's."

"Oh, yes, Rebecca has mentioned you." Elijah sounded friendly, relaxed.

"I'm afraid we have a bit of a situation." Cam hoped the man was stronger than he sounded. "Rebecca was here at my Pack for the bonding ritual between her and Jacob."

Elijah interrupted, a soft chuckle in his voice. "Yes, I know all about that. I hope everything went as planned."

Cam sighed. "Not exactly. The ritual was fine, she and Jacob are now bonded. However, she's gone missing and I don't mean she's went walkabout somewhere. She's been forcibly taken and we're hoping you may be able to help in some way."

A sharp gasp came from the Priest and it was a moment before he replied, "My goodness! I don't quite know what to say."

"Magic was involved." Cam's voice was tightly controlled. "I'm part Witch and I have some unique abilities. I could see the magic in the area but she was drugged, I could smell it. That tells me that whoever took her knew how strong she was and came prepared. Now, Elijah, who would be so upset at Rebecca that they would do something like this? I'll tell you now that she'd already voiced some concerns about Bridget being unhappy at Rebecca's pairing with a Wolf. Bridget has also been avoiding Rebecca's calls, which, to me, is a glaring red light."

"Give me a moment to compose myself." Elijah's response eliciting a small growl of impatience from Cam.

"Time is of the essence." Cam tried to stay civil. "She was taken some hours ago, and we have no idea what's happening to her."

"I see," Elijah replied, his voice a little

harder than it had been before. "I'll see if I can contact Bridget. However, even if I cannot get her on the phone, I most certainly can do a locator spell. It may take me some time to get an exact position though. I will get an idea of the general area much quicker, if that would be of assistance?"

Cam answered immediately, "Yes. If you can get the area to me as soon as possible please. I'll make arrangements to be ready to go at a moment's notice and we can head to where you send us. You can update us as we go."

"I'll do that." Elijah paused for just a second. "I can only imagine what Jacob is going through. Please pass on that I'll do my best to help in any way."

"Thank you." Cam thought on Jacob, knowing that whoever had taken his mate was in serious trouble. "You do realize that I probably won't be able to stop him meting out his own form of justice when we find her, and if she's been harmed in any way at all, then he'll probably kill the person responsible."

"I do understand that. I would probably do the same." Elijah sighed heavily. "Rebecca is very special to me, she's like the daughter I never had, and the thought of someone harming her has me angry as hell. I'm normally a very passive man, Mr. Sinclair, but if anyone's harmed a hair on her head I want them punished in the severest way possible."

"Good to know." Cam relaxed slightly. "I was concerned you wouldn't agree with our ways of dealing with this. I didn't want any fallout of our actions affecting Rebecca."

"Absolutely not. Mr. Sinclair, I'm going to go now and get started. It may be a little while before I call, but be ready to move when I do."

"Don't worry about that. I have vehicles here as well as my jet, if it's a longer journey then we'll use that. I'll let you go now, thank you, and please, call me Cam."

"Goodbye, Cam. We'll talk soon."

Cam stood to return to the living room, Angel's hand on his arm stopping him. "I'm sorry, Cam. This is all my fault."

"No." He shook his head. "It's not your fault. I knew Rebecca would take the first chance she got to help Fergie if she thought she could heal him. Don't blame yourself for this."

"But I do." Angel wrung her hands, her eyes sparkling with unshed tears. "If I hadn't been underhanded about all of this then she wouldn't have been creeping around in the middle of the night."

Cam laid a hand on her shoulder. "Angel, trust me, this is *not* your fault. The only person, or people, responsible are the ones that took her."

"Thank you," she whispered. "I still feel guilty though."

"Maybe the guilt is because of your

deception and not to do with Rebecca at all?" Cam asked, watching as her eyes widened and her face blushed scarlet.

"Yes, possibly," she admitted before going over to help Marie.

~ Chapter 3 ~

"Anything?" Cam asked as soon as he entered the living room.

"Nope," Stracey scowled up at him. "The little bitch isn't answering, either home or mobile."

"That would've been too easy," Jinx grumbled.

"Yes," Stracey agreed. "We'll get her and whoever else she's in league with."

Cam looked at Rory. "Can you go and deal with any Pack stuff for today? I don't want to be worrying about mundane things right now."

Rory stood straighter, nodding. "Sure. I'll get more guards out too. Just in case. Don't worry about anything, Cam. I'll deal with whatever needs attention."

Cam said, "Thank you." His tone heartfelt as Rory disappeared.

Cam's phone started ringing and he answered it quickly. "Yes," he barked, not expecting to hear Elijah's voice again so quickly.

"Sorry," the Priest said quickly. "I've not started my spell yet, but I forgot to mention someone who I think may be involved."

"Go on." Cam listened avidly, hoping Elijah's next words gave them a lead, any lead right now would be good.

"Rebecca had a rather bad ending of a

relationship a while ago. It was a Witch from another coven, but I met him once or twice and I knew he wasn't right for her. She came to that conclusion herself, very quickly I might add, but he wasn't happy about it. He was, now what's the term? Wait, I've got it. He started to stalk her, quite badly. She ended up complaining to his High Priestess and also the local authorities. After that he seemed to stop and I've not heard her mention him since then."

"Really?" Cam perked up. "Who was he and do you have any contact details?"

"I don't have his address or phone number, but his name's Tobias Kane and he lives in Bakersfield. I could call his High Priestess and ask for his details if you like?"

"Yes." Cam smiled. "I'd like that very much. Thank you, Elijah."

"I'll get back to you soon."

Cam hung up as Jinx asked, "What?"

"That was Elijah, the Priest and he's just told me something very interesting." Cam frowned. "Though I'm a little surprised I didn't have all these details. Anyway, Rebecca has an ex, Tobias Kane, from Bakersfield, and long story short, he went all stalkerish on her and she had to report him to his own High Priestess and the local authorities. Elijah didn't like him one bit. Jinx, why didn't we know 'bout this? Surely she would've come to us for help if this guy was bothering her?"

Stracey snorted loudly. "No, she wouldn't. Cam, if she told you 'bout this guy, what would you have done?" She lifted an eyebrow. "Hmm? I know. You woulda gone and found him and beat the crap outta him. Maybe she didn't want that. No, not maybe, she definitely wouldn't want that. You know she's got too big a heart, even if she tries to hide it with all that sassiness."

"She's right, Cam." Jinx shrugged. "Both of us would've gone apeshit if she'd told us."

"I guess you're right." Cam growled. "But hell's teeth, what are friends for if not to look out for each other?"

"There's looking out for each other and then there's the beating the shit outta someone." Stracey chuckled. "She knew you woulda gone with door number two."

"Well, we know now . . ."

"Know what?" Jacob's voice growled as he stood in the open doorway.

"Something about an ex of Rebecca's that she had problems with," Stracey said quietly, sensing the anger that was barely leashed in the large man.

"Fuck!" Jacob cursed, slamming the door behind him. "She mentioned something about that to me but she wouldn't give me any details. Who is this fucker?"

Jacob sat down and they noticed he now had his own laptop in his hands. Opening it up, he

27

quickly started typing. "Give me his details," he ordered.

"Tobias Kane, from Bakersfield, and there must be some kind of paper trail 'cause she reported him to the police." Stracey talked quickly, not wanting to anger Jacob further.

"On it." He worked and spoke at the same time. "Car is a generic sedan. Nothing spectacular about it at all. I checked as soon as I got back with the impressions I took. Now, do we have anything else? If so, tell me now."

Cam sat down next to him. "Bridget isn't picking up but Elijah, the High Priest, is going to help. Says might take him some time but he'll get back to us. He's also going to try and get us this Tobias guy's contact details . . ."

"Don't bother." Jacob snarled. "I've got them here, together with police reports, and everything else about his sorry ass."

"Let me see." Cam strained to look at the screen.

"Rebecca's not the first to report him," Jacob growled. "This guy likes to stalk and I've just found this from when he was in college. A girl reported him for assault. Sexual assault."

Stracey gasped. "What? Shit that is not good."

"No, it's not, 'cause it means when I get my hands on him he is *not* walking away." Jacob's tone was ice cold, deadly and full of malice. "The girl, going from what I've got here, fell apart on the stand and he got off. There's a picture of him leaving court laughing."

Cam shook his head. "He won't be fucking laughing when we finish with him."

"You can say that again," Mac rumbled.

"I've got his details here, Cam, you call." Jacob's face lost some color. "On the off-chance he answers I don't want to tip him off with an opening line of, 'I'm gonna rip you apart' kinda thing. Hold off though, give me your phone."

Cam handed it over and Jacob used a lead to attach it to his laptop before opening up another program. "Here, you can call now, if he does answer I can trace it."

Jinx whistled. "I do *not* want to know where you got that capability from."

"No, you don't," Jacob replied.

Cam looked at the screen then dialed the number, putting it on speaker so everyone could hear they waited with bated breath on someone picking up. On and on it rang, a full minute passed and still nobody answered. "Damn it to hell!" Cam ended the call.

As soon as he did it started to ring. Answering quickly to find Elijah back on the line. "I have the young man's telephone number."

"Thank you, but we managed to obtain it.

We've tried calling, but no answer."

"I see." Elijah paused. "The only thing I can do now is to try and locate Bridget and hope that she is indeed with Tobias. I'll get started on it now but I need to go and get some ingredients for the spell. It's not something I usually do, Cam, but I'll be as quick as I can."

"Thank you." Cam could hear the tension in the man's voice. "We're working some things from our end too. If we find her first then I'll be sure to let you know."

"Thank you." Cam heard Elijah sighing. "I can't tell you how hard this has hit me. I am praying to the Goddess that she is safe and found quickly."

"As are we, Elijah, as are we." Cam looked around, every single person's face grim and full of worry. Except for Jacob's. His was a mask of hate. Cam knew he would have to keep an eye on his friend or he'd completely lose it.

"I'll call as soon as I have something for you," the High Priest replied. "As soon as I can." He reiterated before ending the call.

"Can't you two help?" Jacob looked at Cam and Stracey. "You've got magic, don't you?"

Cam shook his head. "I've never done a locator spell before. Sorry, I wouldn't know where to start with that. Tracking spells, yes, I can do those, but an actual locating one isn't something I can do."

Jacob's eyes spun to Stracey, his head cocked

30

to the side and an eyebrow raised. Stracey held up her hands. "These hands are damn good on a keyboard but I've never been a part of the whole magic scene. I can do basic spells and can sense things but I'm afraid I'm with Cam on this. Locator spells are definitely not in my skill set."

"Fuck!" Jacob cursed before going back to typing furiously on his keyboard. "I'm goin' to find out every last detail about this fucker and then I'm goin' to call in some favors."

"What kind of favors?" Stracey asked.

"The kind that you don't want to know 'bout." Jacob scowled. "The kind that are definitely outside the law."

"I have a few markers I can call in too." Cam stood, going to the door. "I won't be long."

Mac's stomach rumbled loudly, Stracey sniggering as Marie shouted, "Food's on the table."

"Great timing." Mac gave a lopsided grin, heading towards the kitchen with Fergie.

"Jacob . . ." Stracey put her laptop on the floor and stood. "You should eat something."

The glower that he threw her way made her shiver. "Okay, or not," she muttered as she followed Mac, Jinx right beside her.

"Leave him be," Jinx whispered. "I can't even begin to think what he's going through, but I know if you were kidnapped, I couldn't eat a damn thing."

"Just help yourselves." Marie bustled around, laying platters of food in the middle of the table. Plates were already set out as was the silverware, cups, and glasses, jugs of fresh juice and pots of coffee.

Everyone taking their seats and tucking in, Mac's plate already laden with food. Angel snuck glances at Fergie, who blatantly ignored her as he too filled his plate before starting to eat.

They heard Cam talking to Jacob. "I've got a few folks who are looking for this guy. Hopefully, one of them will get back to me soon."

Jacobs answer short and gruff. "Fine."

Cam joined them, taking his seat at the head of the table. "I hope Rebecca's not hurt in any way," he said quietly, obviously not wanting Jacob to hear. "If she is then he'll go crazy. When, and I say when, not if, we find her, then I need you to stay out of his way. He'll go through anyone that's between him and the person responsible. Okay?"

Everyone either nodded or said a quiet "yes." Mac looked over at Cam. "I called Rory and sent a message to Grant, just to let them know what's going on."

Cam nodded as he placed food on his plate. "That's fine, we won't need them to come with us but they should be aware of what's happening."

"What'll happen if she wakens?" Fergie asked. "Won't she be able to deal with them on her

32

own?"

Stracey answered quickly. "Depends. They might have used some sort of magical binding spell. Or, they may not let her wake up just now, until they do have things in place to protect themselves. Only a fool would let Rebecca wake and use her magic. She'd blow them to pieces in a second."

"Magic!" Fergie snarled as Stracey threw him a filthy look.

"Wolves!" she spat back.

"Enough." Cam stopped them before things went any further. "We're all tense and worried but the last thing we need is to argue amongst ourselves. Fergie, I'd like to remind you that I'm part Witch and I use my magic when it's beneficial, to me, or the Pack."

Marie stood behind her son, laying a calming hand on his shoulder. "We know that, Cam. I'm sure Fergie is just upset."

Shrugging off her hand Fergie scowled. "Father hated magic but I guess it has its place. Sorry if I offended either of you."

"We're all a little uptight." Cam acknowledged as Stracey continued to glower at Fergie. "Let's get some food inside us because we don't know when we'll need to make a move. Jinx, can you make sure Marcus is ready? I assume he's still here?"

Jinx swallowed his bacon, nodding. "Yes,

he's staying in the Pack House. He knew Jacob and Rebecca would be going back to LA a few days after their ceremony and didn't see the point in going back and forth."

"Good." Cam poured himself some coffee. "Get him up to speed and tell him we may be leaving at a moment's notice."

"Will do." Jinx grabbed some food and stood.

"Wait—" Cam stopped him. "You can finish your breakfast first. I doubt we'll hear anything in the next ten minutes."

Jinx sat down, piling more food on his plate before tucking back in. Stracey shook her head. "How can you eat so much and still stay slim? I'd be the size of a house if I hate half of what you do."

"Wolf metabolism, darling." Fergie grinned as he poured some maple syrup over his pancakes.

"Not fair," Stracey mumbled as she ate her fresh fruit.

Jacob's voice rumbled and they all could hear him clearly. "Yes! I know that. Don't you think I know I'm asking you to break the law?" He paused a moment before carrying on. "This is my mate I'm talking about and this guy is already on law enforcement radar, so, my *friend*, I'm asking for a favor."

Everyone stopped eating, listening intently to what Jacob was saying. A soft growl was next before he spoke again. "Yes, paper trail, credit card usage. Whatever you can find. I only have my personal laptop with me so I don't have access to all of my programs. You know I wouldn't ask if this wasn't important. Hell, he kidnapped my mate! How more critical could the situation be?"

Cam turned his head, looking through the doorway and watching his friend. Jacob's hand ran through his hair as he listened to whoever he was speaking with. "Okay, thank you. I know I've cashed in the favors you owe but please get back to me as soon as you can."

Jacob hung up, turning to catch Cam watching him. "A friend in the FBI. He's going to try and trace this Tobias guy. If I had my work equipment I could do this myself. Now I'm going to call another friend and see if they'll do the same for Bridget."

"Good luck." Cam turned back to the table, sipping his coffee. "I hope we have something soon. I don't think he'll hold it together if we're not actually doing something."

"I know." Jinx agreed. "If it was me I'd be going crazy sitting around."

"Exactly." Cam looked over at Chastity. "I'm sure I'd be insane by now if you were taken."

She placed a hand on his. "We all know what he's going through, Cam. All of us would feel the same if it were our mate. The best thing we can do is be there for him, support him, and help him find Rebecca and bring her home."

"That's what I plan on doing." Cam squeezed her hand. "I won't rest until we've found her."

"I would expect nothing less from you, Cam." Chastity lifted his hand, placing a soft kiss on the back of it.

"If she's been hurt . . ." Cam's whisper trailed off as his imagination took over. Visions of Rebecca lying hurt and bloody invading his mind as his heart beat like a drum.

"We'll heal her." Stracey spoke so low Cam barely heard her. "If she's hurt we'll heal her. All you guys have to do is find her and bring her home."

"Yeah," Fergie glowered. "Easy peasy."

Stracey's stare was ice cold as she locked eyes with Fergie. "I didn't say that, but some positive thinking goes a long way in bad situations. So, Fergie, cut the sarcasm because this is definitely not the time for it."

"Stracey's right." Mac's voice calm and reasonable, obviously trying to defuse the growing tension between these two. "We need to focus on finding Rebecca and we deal with anything else after that."

"I'm kinda wound tight myself, so, you two," Cam pointed to Stracey and Fergie. "Cut the crap and stop bickering. Fergie, you are not helping the situation."

36

Marie and Angel stopped what they were doing, watching the table as everyone else stopped eating and looked between Cam and Fergie, and back again. It was a long minute before Fergie shook his head. "No, I'm not. Apologies, again. I'm a little uptight myself, what with going to bed a cripple and waking up healed. Especially since I had no say in the matter."

Cam nodded. "I understand that but we need to focus on Rebecca right now."

"I know." Fergie stood up abruptly, his chair flying back. "I'm going to go for some air to help clear my head. I'm sorry, Cam. I won't be long."

Angel took a step toward Fergie but he held his hand up. "No," was all he said as he strode out the back door.

Marie's arm snaked around Angel's shoulders as tears fell from her eyes. She dabbed at them and then ran from the kitchen, sobbing uncontrollably.

"Damn!" Stracey commented to break the awkward silence.

"They need to sort it out between themselves," Cam said as Angel's sobs faded when she ran out the front door.

"Yes," Marie agreed as she went back to work, worry evident in every movement.

~ Chapter 4 ~

As nighttime approached Cam wasn't sure how much longer Jacob could go without erupting in a vicious rage. His contacts had, so far, not found anything they could use. Elijah's call to say that Bridget was using a spell to mask her whereabouts was also a blow that had everyone on edge.

Marie kept up a steady supply of food throughout the day, but Jacob ate nothing. Cam forced him to drink some water but that was all the Wolf would take, saying each time that his stomach was in knots and he would throw up if he even tried to eat.

Cam felt his friend's pain and knew he'd be the same if it were Chastity. Grant had called several times to see if there was any news and each time he had to tell him there was none Cam grew more worried. Every hour that Rebecca was missing meant she was in even more danger and could be getting farther and farther away from them.

Fergie had disappeared for over an hour in the morning, but when he returned he seemed more settled and less argumentative, with everyone except Angel. Every time she tried to speak to him he shook his head and murmured, "Not now."

Everyone could see what it was doing to the woman but they also knew it was something that they had to sort out themselves. Interfering would

38

only make matters worse.

*****

Rebecca tried to move, her entire body aching as she slowly woke. Her legs seemed to hurt even more than the rest of her, at least her upper thighs did. As her brain started to function her heart rate rocketed, fear, terror and anger all mingling inside her.

She forced her eyes to open, seeing a room she was unfamiliar with, her body telling her she was on a bed. Her first thought was to pull as much magical energy inside her so she could defend herself against . . . who? Who was it that had taken her?

Rebecca screwed her eyes closed, trying to remember that moment just before blackness had taken over. Someone had spoken, a voice she knew, one she was, what? Afraid of? Yes. Her eyes flew open as she tried to move a hand to cover her mouth and the low gasp that came from it.

Her hand stayed in place, at her side, and she frowned as she looked down. Her head pounded as she moved it, nausea stampeding up from her stomach. She only just managed to stop herself from throwing up as her eyes saw small, thin bracelets of twine around her wrists.

Making her brain focus, she knew the twine

alone would not suffice to stop her movements. There was only one thing that would do that—magic. And, the person responsible was the one she'd hoped never to see again—Tobias.

"I see you're awake, my darling." His voice making her jump as her stomach roiled again.

Rebecca's eyes flew around the room, finding him sitting on the floor in the corner, his knees drawn up and his arms around them. He'd never looked crazier than he did at that moment. His eyes wide, pupils dilated, the whites speckled with red. Oh no! He'd been using black magic.

The telltale red within his eyes alerting her to just how far he'd fallen. "Why have you brought me here?"

Rebecca's voice rasped, her tone weak, which angered her further. "You do know you are going to be in a heap of shit. Don't you?" She tried again, and her voice was slightly stronger this time.

"Really?" Tobias pushed himself up against the wall, his naked torso looking pink as he stalked towards her. "From who? Nobody knows where we are, baby. As it should be on our honeymoon. Don't you think?"

She couldn't believe her ears as he sat down on the side of the bed and pulled down the sheet covering her. "No!" she groaned as she saw she was naked under the sheet.

"What?" Tobias' fingers trailed down her

throat. "You're my bride, Rebecca, it's my right to touch you, to see you in all your glory, to love you all night long."

"Don't you fucking touch me." Rebecca's anger and fear grew at the same time. "I mean it, Tobias, don't touch me."

"Aaah, dear Rebecca," his hand trailed lower. "You don't quite understand, do you? I already have."

His eyes speared hers as laughter flew from his mouth, spittle landing on her skin as she shook her head furiously. "No, you didn't!"

"Yes," Tobias grinned. "I did."

Rebecca's mind started into freefall, disgust and terror, mingling together. She lowered her eyes, no longer able to look into his insane ones and saw again his chest looked pink. His eyes followed hers. "Oh this?" he rubbed at some of the stain. "Poor little Bridget's, I'm afraid. She had some notion of working to make you understand you needed a Witch by your side and in your bed."

Shaking her head again she murmured, "You hurt her?"

"You could say that." Tobias lifted the finger he'd been rubbing his skin with, and sucked it into his mouth, he licked it clean and smiled. "Hmm, she tastes so good. Pity so much of it landed on the walls and ceiling."

"You're dead," Rebecca spat out. "He'll find

you and he'll kill you."

"Who?" Tobias frowned. "You mean your little puppy dog? No, he won't, nobody knows where I am. No phone to trace, no laptop to access our location. Nothing, nada, zip. We're all alone and I have you to myself. As it should be."

"If he doesn't find us then I'll do it myself." Rebecca struggled again, her movements futile against her bonds.

"Uh, uh, that won't work either, honey." Tobias ran a finger around her wrist. "You are well and truly neutered. No magic for you, my dear."

Tobias leaned over towards her lips. Rebecca tried to move her head but his hand grabbed her chin roughly and held her in place. As soon as his lips were close enough she seized them between her teeth and bit down as hard as she could. His screams of pain like a breath of fresh air, even as his blood dripped into her mouth, she bit harder.

A hand wound around her throat, squeezing her life air from her as she fought to keep his lips between her teeth. She held on for as long as she could before darkness crept towards her and she reluctantly released him. Tobias sat up, madness in his eyes as he clenched a fist and punched her full in the face.

There was a split second of pain before darkness pulled her under again. As she fell towards the blackness, she prayed to the Goddess that her

Wolf would find her.
That, or death.

*****

On and on the hours dragged by, Jacob looking worse by the minute. He went between outbursts of cursing to sitting quietly, his face pale and drawn, as he continued to type on his keyboard. His fingers moving at a speed that belied the size of his hands.

Stracey and Chastity both yawned, again, and Cam stood. "It's time you two got some rest." As Stracey shook her head and Chastity opened her mouth to protest, Cam stopped her. "It's not a suggestion, ladies. We may need you when we bring Rebecca home and you need to rest. Marie," Cam raised his voice so his aunt would hear him. "You too. Some sleep for all of you."

Jinx backed him up. "I agree. You go and rest and if there's any news we'll let you know." He pulled Stracey up. "Go on, baby, you need some sleep."

"I don't want to leave you," she objected, her hand rising to stroke his cheek.

"I know you don't." Jinx leaned his head into her touch. "But, you know I'm right. Go and rest. I promise I'll let you know as soon as we have something."

"Okay," She acquiesced. "But what 'bout you? You all need to rest too."

"We'll grab a nap down here," Cam said as he ushered Chastity towards the stairs.

"Make sure you do," Chastity said as she slowly ascended the stairs.

Stracey was right behind her, glancing over her shoulder at Jinx. "Go," he said, smiling at her reluctance to leave.

"Jacob. . ." Cam started but stopped when his friend almost snarled at him.

"Don't say it, Cam." Jacob didn't look up from his screen. "You know damn well you wouldn't sleep if it was your mate, so don't ask me to."

"True." Cam acknowledged. "I'm going to the office, I'll try and catch a nap there and the rest of you do your best to rest here."

Mac and Fergie lay at opposite ends of one of the large sofas, as Jinx lay on the one Jacob sat on.

Cam must've fallen into a sleep, as he almost toppled from the armchair when his phone started to ring. Stopping himself from tumbling to the floor, he grabbed his phone and answered, "Yes?"

His heart almost thudded out of his chest as one of his contacts started to speak. Cam's lips twitching up as they finally got a lead. "Thanks, can you send me those details?" He got a "yes" and was already on his feet and moving out of the office.

He ran smack bang into a wall of muscle,

almost dropping his phone, as Jacob held his own in his hands. "My contact's just called," Cam said as Jacob grinned.

"Mine too," Jacob said. "Hope it's the same information. What did you get?"

"Leavenworth." Cam waited with bated breath on Jacob's reaction.

"Yup!" Jacob whooped. "We've got 'em!"

"Okay, let's get the guys and we can decide on our course of action." Cam's long legs striding towards the living room.

"There is only *one* course of action," Jacob snarled. "We go, we find, I kill. Simple."

Cam didn't miss the deadly tone and hoped it wasn't going to be a bloodbath. "Wake up!" he shouted as they neared the lounge. "We've got a lead."

Jinx sat up fast, his hands rubbing his eyes as Fergie and Mac awoke a little slower. "Jinx, go get Chastity and Stracey. No, wait, don't bring them down, just tell them we have a lead and we'll phone when we have more information."

"Okay, wait for me before you start discussing things though." Jinx leaped up, rushing upstairs.

Cam's phone vibrated as the information he requested was delivered. Holding his screen towards Jacob who nodded. "Same as what I got," his friend concurred.

45

"Good." Cam looked at Fergie. "You're knowledge of the area is better than ours. Do you know a place called Leavenworth?"

Fergie's eyes widened. "Leavenworth? Jeez, that's less than three hours from here. Quicker if we break the speed limits."

"It may be quicker going by road, Jacob." Cam frowned. "By the time we get Marcus to find out if there's an airstrip nearby and get us clearance, we'll probably be there."

"True." Jacob nodded. "And it's still early so the roads will be quiet, we can drive as fast as we can and hope there's no police around."

Jinx jumped down the stairs. "What've I missed?"

"Okay." Cam took a deep breath. "We think they're in Leavenworth, in a cabin that's been rented by Bridget. It's on the outskirts, pretty remote is what I've been told, but I have the GPS coordinates that we can use to get us there. If we floor it, then we'll be there in under three hours."

Jacob was pacing back and forth, obviously anxious to get under way. Cam held up a hand. "Jacob, we need some supplies, just in case." He turned to Fergie. "A first aid box, water, a blanket, can you get us those now?"

"Sure, give me a minute." Fergie rushed off.

"Jinx, Mac, go and get us some supplies, food, water, etc. We'll need to eat on the go." Cam

46

turned to Jacob. "You've gotta have something. You've not eaten at all and you need to be strong for her."

Jacob shook his head. "I can't, Cam. I just can't."

"You need to drink." Cam frowned. "You need to stay hydrated, and that's not up for argument."

"Water will do me just fine."

"Okay." Cam patted Jacob's arm. "We'll find her, my friend, and we'll bring her home safe and sound."

"I hope so, Cam." Jacob's voice lowered. "I'll die without her."

"I know, Jacob, I know." Cam saw the torture in his friend's eyes. "We won't rest until we've found her."

"Thank you." Jacob pulled Cam in for a bear hug before releasing him when Fergie appeared back.

"Got everything you asked for."

"Okay, we'll take two vehicles." Cam pointed to Mac. "You and Fergie in one, the rest of us in another. We'll use the new arrivals, they'll be faster."

"Thank goodness you thought to upgrade ours," Fergie said. "We haven't bought new ones for years, didn't really need them."

"We have them now," Cam said as they

headed toward the door. "Jinx, move your ass or you'll be left behind."

"Don't you fucking dare!" Jinx roared back, running from the kitchen with two bags in his arms. "Here, take one of these." He almost threw a bag at Fergie as the five large Wolves left the cabin.

The two shiny new Jeeps sat behind the Alpha's cabin, keys on the dash so nobody had to go hunting for them. Jacob moved towards the driver's side of one but Cam stopped him. "I'm driving," he said firmly.

Jacob's face showed he didn't like that idea at all but he didn't argue, grabbing the back door and opening it and jumping in. Jinx got in the front passenger seat, passing over the bag of supplies to Jacob as Cam got in and started the engine. "Buckle up, I'm going to push this baby to the limit and I don't want to be worrying about either of you two."

Cam fastened his own seatbelt and heard the clunk click of the other two as his foot hit the gas and they tore out of the Camp.

"Just try and relax, it's quite a long drive." Cam already inputting the coordinates and asking for the quickest route to be shown in the small screen set into the dash.

"Yeah, right," Jacob replied as Jinx settled down in the leather seat.

"I'll get us there as quick as I can." Cam looked in his rearview mirror, catching Jacob's eyes.

"I know you will," Jacob replied before turning to look out his window.

The darkness beyond showing how early it was. "Damn, what's the time anyway?" Jinx asked.

Cam tapped the screen. "Tells you here and how long it will take for us to get where we're going."

"Half past three!" Jinx exclaimed. "No wonder I'm tired."

"We should get there before six." Cam looked at the information displayed before him. "Maybe quicker. Once we're out onto the highway I'll be pushing this as far as it can go."

"Good." Jacob's voice hard and determined.

"We'll find her." Jinx spoke over his shoulder. "We'll bring her home, Jacob."

"Yes," he nodded. "We will."

As soon as they left the back roads Cam put his foot to the floor, the Jeep flying along the tarmac at breakneck speed. Time seemed to stand still as they drove on into the darkness. They saw very few vehicles on the road, and those that they did see were soon left far behind as Cam tore past them. His eyes flitting to his rearview mirror from time to time to make sure Mac was still behind them.

If he left them in his wake he knew he wouldn't slow down. Nothing would stop him from getting to Rebecca as quickly as he could get them there. Jacob's despair filling the cab as they carried

49

on towards his mate. The miles disappearing as Cam checked his display and saw more than two hours had gone by.

"Less than fifteen minutes, Jacob." Cam checked the map again, the screen showing that he'd need to take a sharp right less than a hundred yards away. His foot finally let up, slowing them so he could make the turn. "Roads look to be no more than dirt tracks from here so I'll need to slow down and it's gonna get bumpy."

Jacob sat up, his neck twisting to look all around. "It's still dark. Hopefully, that will help us."

"Yes," Jinx agreed. "How are we doing this?"

"Quickly," Cam said. "Mac and Fergie can take the back and we'll go in the front. Speed is our biggest ally, and noise, we want to disorient anyone inside. So you can roar and growl all you want. The louder the better."

"I wish we knew what the cabin was like inside." Jacob sat forward. "If it was big enough I'd go Wolf, but if it's not then I won't be able to move."

"Unfortunately, we have no idea, so we go in like this." Cam snuck a glance at his friend. "Plus, we don't want to terrify Rebecca with a horde of Wolves running around."

"My beast is itching to get out, Cam." Jacob struggled around on the seat. "I mean, it's positively fighting to be released."

"I can understand that, but," Cam turned, catching his eye, "you need to control it and use more than brawn if we're to release your mate. A Witch can be a dangerous being, especially one cornered by an angry Wolf. So, Jacob, keep your senses alert and try and not get yourself hurt in the process."

Jacob snorted, then shrugged. "Hey, the only person I see getting hurt is the fucker who's taken my mate."

"Yup," Jinx put in. "I want to get a few hits in on that eejit too."

"We all do," Cam spoke quietly, his knuckles white against the steering wheel.

Jinx looked out the rear window. "Mac's right behind us which is kinda amazing as he doesn't usually drive fast."

"I thought I'd lose him but he's stayed on our tail the whole time." Cam reached to switch off his headlights. "We're nearly there." He slowed right down, the engine quieting as he did so. "I'll stop just up ahead and we'll go the rest of the way in on foot."

Jacob unbuckled his belt. "Cam."

"What?"

"I don't think I've ever said this before in my life." Jacob paused. "But, fuck it all to hell, I'm scared. What if . . ."

"Shut up," Cam ordered. "There *is* no what if. We go in, we find Rebecca, and we bring her

51

home. Nothing else is an option, Jacob."

Jinx reached back, his hand gripping Jacob's arm. "We'll get her, Jacob. As Cam says, nothing else is an option and we *will* bring her back to you."

"Thank you." Jacob sighed. "Cam, do you have clout with the Council?"

Cam slowed to a stop, putting the vehicle in park and turning around. "What?"

"I hope you do." Jacob scowled. "'Cause I don't care what he does, what he says, if Rebecca is in there and so is Tobias . . . I'm ripping him apart."

"I thought as much." Cam bent his head to the side, eyeing up his friend. "I would do the same and I'll deal with it. Elijah has already intimated there won't be a problem from the Witches regarding Tobias, and the Council won't make any noise about what happens here either. They know our ways and what's coming to Tobias is exactly what he deserves."

"Good." Jacob opened his door. "Can we go find Rebecca now, please?"

"We can," Cam stated, his tone deadly as they left the warmth of the jeep.

~ Chapter 5 ~

Mac and Fergie joined them, Mac's face drawn with tension. Jinx smirked. "I take it you didn't enjoy the drive?"

Shaking his head Mac glowered. "No, not especially."

Fergie looked askance at Mac. "He definitely did not enjoy the drive. But, he wouldn't stop so I could take over so I've heard about a hundred 'feck sakes' on the way here."

"I'll bet." Jinx slapped Mac's back.

Jacob let out a low growl. "Can we stop with the chatting and go do what we came here to do?" He looked hard at Mac and Fergie. "You remember, don't you? Rebecca? My mate?"

They could all see the blush on Mac's face, even in the pre-dawn darkness. "Sorry," he said as Cam took over.

"The cabin is up ahead, couple of hundred yards." Cam pointed to Mac and Fergie. "You two take the back and we'll go in the front. We're not hanging around to scope it out. We're going in hard and fast, with as much noise as you can muster. Okay?"

"Sure," Fergie said as Mac nodded vigorously.

"Good. You go ahead first as you need to get to the back before we go in." Cam moved to let them pass. "Go."

All of them took off at a run, using their Wolf speed to fly along the track. Fergie was out front with Mac on his tail, Jacob right behind. Cam was next with Jinx protecting the rear as their eyes saw a cabin's outline coming into view.

"Too fucking small," Jacob cursed as they neared the building.

A slight lightening of the darkness alerting them to dawn approaching fast. No lights shone from inside the cabin as Fergie and Mac tore around the side and Jacob barged straight for the door. His massive frame, together with his speed and Wolf strength, obliterated the wood as he barreled inside, roaring like a madman.

Cam right behind him as Jacob pulled up short, Cam banging into his back. "What is it?" he asked, as Jacob let out a long low groan.

Cam's heart thudded in his chest as he looked around the small living room. His nose the first sense to alert him as the unmistakable scent of blood invaded his nostrils. As Cam tried to process what was before him, Jacob took off, screaming Rebecca's name over and over.

"What the fuck?" Jinx was beside Cam as they looked around them.

There was blood everywhere, absolutely everywhere. The walls were splattered with it, the floor soaked in it, the ceiling coated in it, the dark red stark against the white paint. Jinx pointed to the corner. "Cam, oh my fuck, that's not. . ."

Cam belted over, dropping to his knees to turn over the crumpled body. It was completely saturated in blood, slick and still wet, the hair so dark with it that he had no clue as to the original color. Cam held his breath as the body flipped over and he looked down into the still open, dead, blue eyes. "Thank you," he threw up to the Goddess. "It's not her."

Jinx nodded and it was then that all hell broke loose. Jacob howled in anger, a door ripped from its hinges and flying back into the living room. Jinx only just managing to dodge the deadly force before it knocked him flying. Cam rose, taking off as quick as his powerful legs could carry him, towards the noise.

Jacob had a man in his grip, his large hand around his throat, squeezing the life from him as he banged his head against the wall, again and again. Incomprehensible noises erupting from the Wolf's throat as the man's legs kicked futilely. Cam stopped and waited. There was no way he was getting between Jacob and Tobias Kane.

There was no doubt who it was that was in Jacob's death grip. They'd all seen his picture and this was most definitely the man. Cam sent his senses out, scenting more fresh blood from the room at the end of the hallway—Rebecca's.

He would know her scent anywhere and he struggled to stop himself rushing forward. He even took a step before Jinx's hand stopped him. "Wait," his Beta said quietly.

"I can smell her," Cam groaned, knowing he couldn't get past Jacob without some serious trouble.

"She's his mate, Cam." Jinx kept a hold of his arm. "You may have known her a lot longer, but, you need to wait and let him get to her first. There's no other danger here. He's got his hands on the only threat to her and from what I can see he's taking care of that nicely."

"Do you know how hard it is to stand here when every fiber of my being is telling me to get to her?"

"Yes," Jinx nodded. "I do. The simple fact is we can't."

Cam growled, his urgency to get to his friend growing by the second. Jacob's loud roar bringing his attention back to the fight in front of him. Jacob was shaking the body like it was a toy, Tobias' eyes almost bugging out of their sockets.

Jacob roared one last time, pulled his free hand back, obviously putting every last bit of strength into a forward punch. They all heard the bones snap, break under the power of Jacob's blow, a loud popping sound alerting them to the destruction of the heart that lay behind those bones. As blood spurted from Tobias' mouth, Jacob released

56

his stranglehold and allowed the limp body to fall to the floor.

Cam stepped forward as Jacob ran towards the room at the end, pushing the door open with such force that it flew back, the handle embedding within the wall and staying there. The choked groan from Jacob as he fell to his knees beside the bed almost had Cam's eyes filling with tears.

"Keep everyone out." Cam pushed Jinx back, away from the sight within the room.

Cam tugged the door from its place within the wall and closed it gently before going over towards Jacob. He carefully made his way, talking calmly to make sure his friend knew he was there and no threat.

"Jacob, nobody else is coming in." Jacob's hands moved all over Rebecca's body, touching the bruises and marks covering her pale skin. "Nobody will see her like this. I'll send the others away and you and I will take her home. Okay?"

Cam could see she'd been abused, his anger like molten lava within him. "We'll help her, make her better. Get her through this."

Jacob's head spun around. "You know what he's done. Don't you?"

Cam nodded, his voice sad as he answered, "Yes, Jacob. I know."

"Of course you do." Jacob stared up at Cam. "It reeks in here of what he's done. What do I do,

Cam? How do I help her through this?"

"I'm not sure," Cam admitted. "But, whatever it takes, we'll do it. I'll help in any way I can and I'll get her any professional support she needs. We'll do it, Jacob. You're not alone in this, neither of you are alone in this. We'll do it together."

"Just wait here for now." Cam went to the door. "I'll only be a moment."

Cam opened the door and slipped through into the hallway. Jinx and Max standing about halfway along. "Where's Fergie?"

"Outside, checking the perimeter and making sure there's no other danger." Jinx nodded toward the door behind Cam. "Is she okay?"

Cam didn't answer but gently shook his head. "Jinx, I need you to contact the Council and get them to come and clean this up. You'll need to give them a report of what's happened and if they give you any problems, then, shit, tell them I'll deal with them direct in a day or two. I have other things to sort out now."

"Sure," Jinx said, raising an eyebrow in query.

"I also need you to go back with Mac." Cam shook his head when he saw Jinx ready to ask why. "Jacob and I will bring Rebecca back. Can you ask Stracey to be available, in case we need her?"

"Of course." Jinx frowned. "You're worrying me, Cam."

"I know." Cam shrugged. "I'm sorry, but this is the way it's got to be. I won't say more, just do as I ask."

Mac stepped forward. "Cam, is there anything I can do? Anything at all?"

Cam shook his head, sadness in his eyes. "No, thanks for offering, but no. We just need some privacy right now and I'd appreciate it if you'd get the jeeps brought up here, with one set up right at the front door and open so we can take her straight in."

"We'll do that now." Mac whirled around, jogging away.

"It's bad, isn't it?" Jinx whispered.

Cam knew his eyes answered for him.

"We'll be leaving soon, so if you could make sure the vehicle's all set and then if you could wait out back?"

Jinx sighed, "Yes, whatever you need. Are you sure I can't help?"

"No." Cam turned away. "Not this time, Jinx."

Cam heard Jinx curse as he returned to the bedroom. "We'll be set to go soon."

Jacob held Rebecca in his arms, the sheet that had covered her was now wrapped tightly around her. "Good, 'cause I *need* to get out of this room. Cam, I want this place burned to the ground. I don't want a single thing left standing."

"If that's what you want, then I'll make sure

of it." Cam walked over, sitting on the bottom of the bed. "I'll pay whatever sum, to whomever it takes, but it can't be done now, Jacob. We need the evidence of what he's done. Not just to Rebecca, but to that girl out there too."

"Fine," Jacob snarled. "When that stuff's over, can we do it then?"

"Yes." Cam's head fell to the side, his own pain deep inside him as he looked at Jacob. "I promise, when the Council has everything they need, this place won't stand for another day."

A soft knock on the door preceded Jinx's voice. "Car's out front."

"Thank you, we'll be out in a moment," Cam answered softly.

"Jacob, are you ready?"

Jacob stood, holding his mate close to him as he nodded. Cam opened the door, checking it was clear before leading his friend out to the waiting jeep. Once Jacob was settled in the rear with Rebecca still in his arms, Cam got in, started the engine and drove away. When he looked in the rearview mirror, Mac, Jinx and Fergie stood watching them leave.

"What if he's done too much damage?" Jacob murmured.

"She's strong." Cam sounded far more confident than he felt. "We'll make sure she's okay. Trust me, Jacob."

"Okay," Jacob sighed. "I wish I'd tore him limb from limb, slowly."

"I know you do," Cam replied. "So do I."

Silence was their partner for most of the journey, neither knowing quite what to say. That was until they were about half an hour away from Camp and Rebecca started to stir in Jacob's arms. Her head flew from side to side before she screamed, loud, long and hard.

"Nooooooooooo!"

Jacob tried to soothe her. "Becca, baby, it's me, Jacob. I've got you. You're safe, honey, I promise you're safe."

Cam watched in the mirror as Rebecca's eyes flew open, terror on her face. "Jacob? Is that really you or has that fucker used more magic on me?"

"It's me, I promise."

Rebecca didn't look as if she believed him. "If it's you then prove it. Tell me what you said when you caught me reading that book."

Jacob ran a finger down the side of her face. "I told you 'I'm no Mr. Grey. I'm better.'"

A long sob escaped her. "Yes, yes you did. Now, can you remove the twine he put around my wrists? They're magical and I can't move with them, or perform any fucking magic."

Jacob quickly tore the thin twine from her arms. "Better?" he asked, still holding her close.

"Not sure." Rebecca's face collapsed, tears

filling her eyes. "He did stuff, Jacob. While I was knocked out, he *did* stuff."

Cam's heart almost broke at her voice, full of pain, hurt, and distress. Jacob hushed her. "Shhh, I know baby, I know. Becca, you don't need to think about that now. We'll get you home and cleaned up and then you need to eat something and get some rest. We can deal with anything tomorrow, or the day after, hell, whenever you want, babe."

"I hate him." Her voice was now stronger, full of her loathing. "Did you catch him?"

Jacob nodded. "Yes. I caught him. He won't harm anyone again, Becca. Never again."

"Good! I hope he suffered." Rebecca's hand grabbed his shirt. "Oh god, he killed Bridget. He was covered in her blood."

Cam spoke up, "We found her, Rebecca. The Council are on their way to deal with the bodies."

"She was just a stupid little girl," Rebecca sighed. "She'd always gotten her own way and she got it into her head I had to pair with a Witch. She was so foolish thinking that this would turn out the way she wanted, and now she's dead. Poor girl."

Cam knew what was coming, and he only had to wait for a moment before Jacob growled. "She's not a 'poor girl.' She helped him take you. She was probably the one that put the idea into his head, Becca."

"Maybe, probably, but she didn't deserve to

die like she did."

"Always thinking of others." Jacob pulled her up, letting his lips gently brush hers. "My Becca, you are too kind at times."

"Shhh," Rebecca snuggled into his arms. "Don't tell anyone, or I'll lose my rep."

Cam sneaked another look and saw her eyes slowly closing as Jacob rocked her softly. "That's it, baby, go back to sleep." Her mate coaxed as they neared home, and safety.

~ Chapter 6 ~

Cam paced back and forth in front of the cabin where Jacob and Rebecca were staying. It'd been a full week since they'd rescued her and he'd only seen her a couple of times. Every time he arrived to visit, Jacob would say that she didn't want to see anyone, including him.

He didn't know how long he could go without barging in and making sure that she was okay. Stracey had been in a few times and each time assured Cam that Rebecca was making progress, but hell, he needed to see for himself.

Cam rapped on the door, again, then commenced his pacing. His ire rising until the door opened slowly. "What the hell is the time?" Jacob growled.

"It's morning. How's Rebecca?" Cam growled back.

"She's a lot better. . ."

Cam interrupted, "So I can see her?"

"She's still asleep, Cam." Jacob came out, standing outside and staring as Cam glowered.

"I promise you she's getting better," Jacob said softly, his tone a little apologetic.

"So you say." Cam grumbled. "But I need to see her for myself. I'm going out of my head with worry."

"What can I say?" Jacob shrugged. "She's

not wanted to see anyone. It's not just you, Cam."

"I *need* to see her." Cam almost ordered, barely restraining himself.

"Don't." Jacob snarled. "I'm not a full member of your Pack so you can't do the Alpha thing with me. Don't even try it or we'll have a problem."

Cam stepped forward, his emotions running high and ready to escalate things, when the door creaked. He and Jacob spun towards it as Rebecca stuck her head out.

"What the hell's going on? A pissing contest?"

Cam smiled. "Hi, I just needed to see you were okay."

"I'm fine." Rebecca looked between the two men. "Well, I was before I was so rudely wakened. Cam, come back this afternoon and we can talk. Jacob, get your big Wolf ass back inside and get me some coffee."

Chuckling, Cam turned to walk away. "See ya later." He threw over his shoulder as Rebecca's arm snaked out to haul Jacob inside.

Cam started to whistle as he made his way back to the Alpha cabin. That was one thing he'd been dreading out of the way. Now, he had another. He and Fergie were going to have to talk. The tension between them rising as the week had progressed.

It wasn't as if he was unsympathetic to

65

Fergie's feelings and Chastity had come up with a solution. However, Cam wasn't sure if he wanted her resolution and if he didn't then that meant he and his cousin had a huge problem.

As he strode along, whistling, he saw Chastity coming towards him. His heart flared to life when he looked at her, her long blonde hair billowing out behind her as she started to run. As soon as she was close enough she launched herself into his arms. "Where were you?" she grumbled. "I hate it when you're not in bed when I wake up."

"Sorry," Cam apologized. "I needed to check up on Rebecca."

"Did you see her?" Chastity asked, placing a kiss on his cheek as she struggled to get back on her feet.

Cam held her tight for a moment longer before releasing her. "Sort of. She stuck her head out the door to tell me and Jacob off for waking her and then ordered him to make her coffee."

Chastity giggled. "Seems like Rebecca is back."

"Yes," Cam agreed. "I think so. I'm going back this afternoon to have a chat with her. I'll see how she is then, but I'm hopeful that she's on the mend."

Chastity's head leaned over to the side, looking up at him through her lashes. "You never did tell me what happened."

"No." Cam shook his head. "And I never will. That's not my story to tell."

"Must've been bad if you won't tell me anything." Chastity took his hand as they resumed walking.

"No comment," Cam replied softly.

"Well, I hope she *is* better and that you can stop worrying about her."

Cam stayed silent, wondering if he'd ever stop worrying about his friend. Probably not. After her ordeal he was scared for her. Scared it would change her, who she was, the person he loved dearly; the sassy Witch with a heart of gold.

"Anyway . . ." Cam tugged her hand. "Are you ready for our trip? We need to leave later today, early evening will be fine, but I need to be in LA tomorrow morning for a meeting. Then we need to go shopping for you and there's the charity ball in three days. You ready for that too?"

Chastity nibbled on her bottom lip for a moment. "I suppose. I guess I'm just nervous about it all. Pack life I'm used to. A billionaire's lifestyle with balls and gowns, not so much."

"Stracey and Jinx will be there and I'm sure you'll do just fine." Cam could feel her nervousness. "You'll be like a breath of fresh air, honey. Not one of the women who bitch and moan, who try to get their hooks into men just because they're rich. You're so far removed from them that it's like looking at the sun after a long, dark night."

"I just hope I don't make a fool of myself, or you." Chastity stopped, forcing Cam to halt and look at her. "Cam, I think I'd die of embarrassment if I did something really stupid like fall over in front of everyone."

"What?" Cam frowned. "Why the hell would you fall? You're one of the most graceful women I've ever met. You move so elegantly, with poise, and agility, so why would you think that?"

"I've never, and I mean never, worn heels. What if I can't walk in them?"

Cam laughed, his eyes twinkling as he tugged her onward again. "We just need to make sure the shoes you get are comfortable, and you can practice before we go out. I can't pretend to understand how women manage to walk in what they put on their feet. All I know is that there seems to be some kind of innate ability to do so. Do not worry, please. The ball is supposed to be fun, not an ordeal, but if you want to leave at any time, then all you need do is ask. Okay?"

"Sure," Chastity mumbled.

"Is breakfast ready? I'm famished," Cam asked as they walked up the stairs to the door.

"Yes, Marie's in the kitchen working, as usual."

"Good." Cam pushed the door open and led her to the kitchen. "Morning," he said as he took his seat.

"Good morning." Marie smiled. "Breakfast is ready but if there's something else you want, just ask."

"Nope." Cam started to pile food on his plate. "You've got it covered."

Chastity filled her plate and poured both her and Cam some coffee. "Morning, Marie. Where's Angel?"

Marie shrugged. "I'm not sure. She's usually here by now but she's not arrived. I hope everything's okay. I know they were planning on having a talk, about, well, you know what about."

Chastity looked to Cam and raised an eyebrow. "I see," Chastity said. "I hope everything's okay too. I'm sure it will be, don't worry, Marie."

"I'm a mother, it's my job to worry." Marie smiled and then carried on bustling around.

"So—" Chastity sipped her coffee. "Stracey and Jinx are now living in Stracey's house, which is near yours. Is that right?"

Cam nodded, mumbling around his food. "Yes," he swallowed and carried on, "My house is on its own land with security wall, gates, and CCTV. Stracey has a small bungalow nearby, still on my property but far enough away for privacy. It's only got two bedrooms but I guess that'll do them unless they start to have kids, then we'll need to look at adding on to it for them."

"Might be worth doing now." Chastity looked for the OJ and poured herself some. "What I mean is, it's kinda late to start building when she's already pregnant. I know I'd hate for that to be going on around me if I was carrying a child. So, what if you add a couple more rooms onto it now and that way when they start a family it's all set."

"What if they don't want kids?" Cam asked.

"Jinx is a Wolf, he's gonna want kids. I know Stracey is part Witch, but I'm pretty sure she'll want kids too. She's gaga over Jinx and when that happens it usually means the woman wants that person's child. However, maybe you should ask their opinion on it, after all, it's their life."

"True." Cam smirked. "Jeez, can you imagine little Jinx's running around?"

"Yes," Chastity grinned. "I can."

"Well, it won't be for some time. I hope anyway." Cam carried on eating, pondering the thought of children in their future. Not something he would've thought possible only a short time ago.

"What you got planned for today?" Cam asked between mouthfuls.

"I'm going over to Wild Flower, apparently Mason wants to show me something."

"Mason?" Cam put his coffee down. "What's he wanting to show you?"

"I don't know, but he's excited about it, or so Logan said." Chastity looked over at Cam. "You okay about Grant leaving today?"

Cam shrugged. "I'm not sure. He stayed longer than he'd planned and it's been nice having him around, but he needs to get back to his own Pack. Though, I'm not sure how everyone's going to react to Shelly being with him. I told him to call and warn our parents but he said he wants to surprise them."

"Oh, I'm not sure if that's a good idea or not." Chastity pushed her plate away before finishing her juice.

"Me neither. Our father isn't good with surprises and this one is huge. I just hope he doesn't let the old man try and bully Shelly."

Chastity laughed, taking a moment or two to reply. "Shelly is more than capable of standing up for herself. She's feisty and strong, Cam. I'm sure she'll be okay."

"Hmm, you've not met my father. He can be rather . . . tough."

"I also don't think Grant will let anyone hurt her. They are so in tune with each other that he'll soon know if anyone's upsetting her." Chastity laid a hand on his arm, softly rubbing up and down. "Try and not worry too much. But, I was wondering, I know that some Packs are still stuck in the old ways. You know, where a new member has to prove themselves, and I was wondering if she'd have any of that to go through? If so then I think she should be warned so she can prepare herself."

Cam shook his head. "No, we've not done that for many years. Well, unless someone challenges a newcomer that is. But that's so rare I can't remember the last time it was done."

"Good. Moving to Scotland is a huge enough deal without worrying about having to put up with something like that. Anyway, I've gotta go, I told Mason I'd be over first thing."

"Let me know what the big secret is when you get there. I'm curious."

Chastity picked her plate, cup and glass up, taking them to the dishwasher but Marie grabbed them from her. "I'll do that, off you go."

"Thanks." Chastity smiled. "Okay, Cam, I'll let you know and I won't be too long. I'll be back before lunch."

"Fine." Cam stood, leaving his plate on the table. Chastity nodded towards his things and he shrugged before picking them up. As soon as he did Marie rushed over, taking them from him. Cam raised an eyebrow as Chastity came over and reaching up, pecked him on the cheek. "I'm planning on having a meeting with Fergie later this morning. Wish me luck," he whispered.

"Good luck." Chastity's eyes locked with his. "Try to not lose your temper, please."

"Moi?" Cam feigned indignation. "Never."

"Yeah, sure, whatever you say." Chastity

walked away. "Just think how you'd feel if it were you." She flew over her shoulder as she left.

Cam watched her as she disappeared, his eyes keenly on her jean clad ass. "Damn," he muttered before heading towards the office.

*****

"How could you?" Fergie sneered. "We had everything. The main thing being the trust between us and you go and throw that away. Tell me, Angel, why?"

Angel's head stayed bowed as she sat on the sofa, her hands wringing in her lap. "I'm sorry, Fergie. You know how sorry I am."

"I understand you're sorry but that doesn't take away how you went about doing this." Fergie stomped to the window then back again, stopping in front of his mate. "Look at me, Angel, look at me."

Angel's head lifted, her sorrow clear in her eyes. "What do you want me to say? You know why I did it and I don't regret it. I don't!"

"Was I not enough for you?" Fergie asked, anger clear in his tone.

"What?" Angel looked up, surprise and hurt in her eyes. "Why would you ask me that? I love *you*, mon amor. I didn't do this for me! I did it for you!"

"Maybe I wasn't man enough for you being in that fucking chair? Is that it?"

Angel stepped closer, her hands balled in fists as she glowered up at him. "Don't you dare say that! I would love you no matter what! I did this for you, Fergie. You were dying inside! You were shriveling up and dying. I could *not* stand by and watch that. I love you too much."

Fergie scowled, his anger rising again. "You lied, you deliberately did something that I said I didn't want."

"For all the wrong reasons!" Angel shouted back up at him. "Why would you not want to be healed when it was easy to be done? I've never understood that. It's madness."

"You know perfectly well how my father hated magic."

Angel stood, anger giving her strength. "Your father is gone, mon loupe, and yet you still didn't seek help. Why?"

Fergie turned, walked away and stopped at the window, staring out at the Camp, his voice barely a whisper. "Because now we're in the position of my beast wanting to challenge Cam, that's why."

Angel rushed over and stood beside him. "You don't need to do that."

Fergie didn't look at her, continuing to stare outside. "I'm not sure I can stop it. Angel, this is *my* Camp, *my* Pack, and how do I reward the man that saved us all? I challenge him to a fight for Alpha. Yay, go me! Ain't I the ungrateful ass?"

"Fergie, he'll understand. He knew the moment he saw you walking that things would have to change." Angel tugged on his sleeve, forcing him to look at her. "He's a businessman and a great Alpha, but you're right, this is your Pack. But, my love, you do not have to fight him. All you need to do is talk to him. I'm sure you can sort something out."

"He's taken to the role like a duck to water." Fergie stared down at her. "He's not going to give it up without a struggle."

Fergie sighed, turning away briefly before returning his gaze back to pin her in place. "That wasn't the question though. Was it?"

Angel held her hands up. "I can't say more than I already have. I love you. More than you'll ever know. I knew if I did what I planned that I might lose you. I knew that. But," Angel shrugged. "It was worth it. To see you as the strong Wolf you always were but had to hide behind sarcasm and jokes because you were stuck in that chair. I'm telling you, my mate, I'd do it again to help you walk once more. To give you back your pride I'd walk over broken glass so deceiving you was far easier."

Fergie shook his head. "Damn, Angel, you know how much I adore you, but I'm not sure I'd ever do something like that. Not behind your back."

"I did what I had to do." Angel turned away, her shoulders slumped. "If I've lost you then so be it. Just let me know so I can make arrangements."

Fergie stalked over, grabbing her shoulder and spinning her around. "What arrangements?"

Angel let a hand move to cover the one that still held her in place. "Fergie, mon loupe, if you can't forgive me, if I've lost you, then I'll leave. I can't possibly stay here and see you every day. It would be like sticking a knife in my guts over and over. I couldn't take that, not every day."

Fergie's heart did a hard stutter in his chest. "You'd really leave?" His voice barely even a whisper.

"I'd have to. For my own sanity, Fergie, you're my life, mon amor, my whole life. If you can't forgive me. If we can't get past this. Then, I'll have no choice."

Fergie pulled away, horror in his voice, as he paced around. "You wouldn't."

Angel looked up at him. "Yes, I would. You're my all, mon loupe. I could never stay here and not be with you. It would destroy me. But," she gave him a small smile. "It would be worth it. Seeing you like this. Tall, strong, confident, yes, my love, it's definitely worth it."

"Fuck!" Fergie stomped over, pulling her roughly into his arms. "Don't even say something like that! My heart almost stopped, my Angel. Don't ever, and I mean ever, say you'd leave again."

"Darling," Angel squirmed. "You're

squashing me."

Fergie loosened his grip, just a little. "I guess we need to make up, don't we?"

Angel smirked. "Well, that depends. Are you talking about how we usually 'make up'? If so, then the answer's yes."

"Good." Fergie bent down, scooping her up into his arms. "We won't talk about this again. It's over. Done with. Okay?"

"More than okay." Angel laughed as he carried her to their bed.

~ Chapter 7 ~

Cam was just finishing up a conference call when there was a knock on the door. "Come in," he said, closing down the laptop and rolling his chair back to stretch his legs.

Fergie appeared in the door, looking extremely uncomfortable, and more than a little on edge. "You don't need to knock, Fergie." Cam was surprised, usually his cousin would walk right on in.

"I heard you talking business. I didn't want to interrupt."

"Thanks, but it's done now." Cam stood, going over to the two armchairs set around the fireplace. "Come and sit down, Fergie, I think we've a lot to talk about."

Fergie strode over and sat down but didn't say anything. Instead he looked at the fireplace intently, his agitation clearly showing. "I know it's still early, but do you want a drink?" Cam asked, wondering if it would help smooth the discussion that was looming.

"No, I'm good." Fergie sighed. "This is awkward, isn't it?"

"Just a bit." Cam agreed. "It's not easy for either of us, Fergie. Here we are in a situation neither of us envisaged."

"Tell me about it." Fergie sighed again. "I was the one that begged you to take over. You didn't want to, I saw that, but I begged and you did what was best for the Pack. You have to know how grateful I am for that, Cam. Don't you?"

"Yes." Cam also sighed, knowing this wasn't going to be an easy conversation. "I didn't want to be Alpha, you knew that. I fought against it so damn hard, Fergie, so when you forced my hand, for the sake of the Pack, I was surprised when I began to enjoy it. No, that's wrong, I love being Alpha. Must be in the DNA or somat."

"I know what you mean." Fergie looked over at Cam for the first time and Cam could see an Alpha staring back at him.

"I'm not sure what we do now. All I know is that I don't want bad blood between us." Cam watched Fergie's face closely for any sign of animosity. "Chastity has come up with a solution and it may be that I take that course of action. However, I won't be rushed or forced into it. I don't make these kinds of decisions lightly and I know that's probably not what you want to hear right now, cousin, but it's all I can give you."

"The last thing I want is bad blood, Cam. Not after everything you've done for me and my family, as well as the Pack." Fergie looked away. "But, I have to say this, my DNA is kicking in too and my need to be Alpha is growing by the day. How long do you think you need?"

"I'm going back to LA later today, I'll be

away for about a week at least, possibly longer. I'll do my thinking and decision making in that time and we'll talk again when I get back. I'd like you to take over while I'm gone though. Is that acceptable?"

Fergie stood. "As we don't want things going bad between us, I guess it'll have to be."

"Wait—" Cam also stood, holding his hand out. "Can I ask, is everything okay with you and Angel?"

Fergie shook Cam's hand, using a little too much strength for it to be purely friendly, before he answered. "Yes, we sorted things between us. Thanks for asking."

"She only did what you would've done if the situation were reversed. What any of us would do for our mate."

"I think you're right." Fergie conceded before turning to leave. "I'll take care of things while you're gone and we'll talk when you get back."

"Good," Cam said, a long exhale escaping when his cousin had left. *That went better than I'd thought.*

Staying in the office to take care of some business, including a conference call with Stracey and Mr. Akiyama regarding the Japanese deal, the morning disappeared. Chastity's soft knock before entering causing him to quickly check the time. "Hi, you're back. What was it Mason was so desperate to show you?"

Chastity grinned. "Not telling, it's a surprise. All I'll say is it's beautiful and I think you'll like it."

"Really?" Cam stood, going around the desk to grasp her to him. "You won't even give me a hint?"

"Nope. My lips are sealed." Chastity motioned with her fingers in a parody of closing his lips.

"Hmm, I'm not sure I like my mate having secrets with another Wolf."

Chastity scowled. "Don't be silly and don't go all jealous Alpha, it doesn't suit you."

"Jealous?" Cam scowled back. "Don't think I've ever been jealous before. It's kinda new, and weird, so let's just call it concern."

"Whatever." Chastity reached up to kiss his cheek. "Lunch is ready and Grant and Shelly are here. They're gonna eat with us and then Logan is taking them to the airport."

"Is it that time already?" Cam checked the time again. "Damn, that's come around too darn fast."

"I know." Chastity could obviously feel Cam's sadness. "Hopefully it won't be too long 'til you see each other again."

"Yes, let's go, I need to tell them something." Cam took her hand and led them through the kitchen.

"Hello, Cam." Grant smiled, getting up to

hug his brother.

"Hi, I'm sorry, I didn't realize the time or I would've come out earlier."

"No worries, brother." Grant slapped his shoulder. "I know how busy you are."

Everyone took their seats before filling their plates with the food already laid out. "Thank you, Marie," Cam said as Marie blushed.

"You're welcome. If it's okay I'll pop out for a bit. I want to go and talk to Angel and make sure everything's okay."

"Of course." Cam nodded.

As Marie opened the back door she stopped, turning and giving a small wave. "Goodbye, Grant, Shelly. I hope to see you for a visit sometime soon."

"Bye." Both Grant and Shelly replied as Marie disappeared.

"So, are you all set to meet the parents, and the Pack?" Cam asked Shelly as she sipped on some water.

"I'm not really sure," she admitted. "I guess I'm as ready as I'll ever be."

"One piece of advice, if I may?" Cam directed this to Grant who nodded.

"Don't take any shit from our father. Stand up to him and let him know you are the Alpha's mate, the Alpha She-Wolf, and you only take orders from Grant."

Grant chuckled. "Yeah, that is good advice."

Shelly's face looked worried. "You're scaring me, Cam. Is he that bad?"

"It depends." Cam shrugged. "If you let him know from the get go how things stand then I think you'll get along fine. He just needs reminding that he can't control everyone around him."

"Okay, I'll do my best." Shelly still looked a little worried.

"As for mother, she'll be fine. Don't worry. As soon as she sees the depth of feeling between you two then she'll be happy."

"Thanks, Cam, I hope so." Shelly smiled at Grant, her love shining in her eyes.

"Don't worry, mo runsa, I'll make sure nobody makes you uncomfortable. And, there's Blayne too, he's American, though he's been with our Pack for over fifty years now. He fought in the last war and was stationed in Scotland. When the war was over he decided to come back to live. I can't figure out how he's not lost his accent, even a little bit, but he hasn't. Talks with a different one to yours but it's still American."

"Blayne? Where's he from?" Shelly looked interested in this snippet of information.

"I think he's from the Deep South, maybe Mississippi, or round 'bout that area." Grant frowned, obviously trying to remember. "He said he came to Scotland because, at the time, there was a lot of bigotry and he hadn't found that when he was stationed there. So he came back, and he's never left. He has a mate, Flora, and two kids, Bridley and Callie."

Shelly nodded. "Oh, I see, yeah, we certainly had our share of problems in the past. Though any Packs I lived in didn't bother with that sort of stuff. We were all Wolves, no matter anything else."

"Exactly," Grant agreed. "It's hard for us to understand as we never looked, either then or now, on anyone other than being part of the Pack. Anyway, he's one of our Americans and we have another, Bradley, or as he keeps insisting, Brad. He's only been with the Pack for about ten years but he's a hard worker and a bit of a joker."

"So I won't be the only one talking in a strange accent?" Shelly asked, obviously still anxious.

Cam grinned. "Hell no. The Pack has some folks from all over. Last time I checked there was a French woman, a German guy, and oh yeah, isn't there that Aussie?"

Grant nodded. "Yeah, they are all still there, so don't worry about how you talk. It's not an accent that folk's bother about, it's what you say that's important."

"I see." Shelly looked between Cam and Grant. "And what exactly is it I should be saying?"

"That's a good question." Cam looked to Grant. "Brother, care to enlighten us?"

84

Grant gave a cheeky smile. "Well, how much you love and adore me, of course!"

Shelly swatted his arm. "I'm so not going to go around saying that. You'll end up with a big head."

"Can't hurt a guy for trying." Grant laughed as Shelly punched his arm.

"Yeah, I can." She laughed back.

Cam remembered what he wanted to tell his brother. "Grant, I'm sorry I can't give you the jet to fly home but I'm going to be using it. However, I have made sure you two are flying first class. That means you can also use the First Class Lounge at the airport and you should be well taken care of there, and on the flight."

Grant's eyes widened. "First Class huh? Well that's just dandy! Thanks, Cam."

"I've never flown First Class before." Shelly laughed, clapping her hands in glee. "I'm looking forward to this, oh, can I have champagne on the flight?"

Cam grinned. "Of course. I've already ordered a bottle to be chilled and waiting for you upon boarding."

Grant reached over, slapping Cam's shoulder. "Way to go, Cam."

"It's the least I could do and I promise I'll come and visit soon." Cam shrugged. "Well, maybe not soon, but I certainly won't leave it as long between visits this time."

"You better not." Grant emphasized by cocking an eyebrow. "If you do then I'll get dad a flight over to visit you!"

"Don't you fucking dare!" Cam cursed. "That's not funny, Grant."

"It is from where I'm sitting." Grant joked.

"Sorry to interrupt," Logan's voice interrupted. "But we need to leave now."

"So soon?" Cam queried. "We've not finished lunch yet."

"Afraid so, Alpha," Logan reiterated.

"Damn." Cam glowered. "Mo bhràthair, guess we need to say goodbye."

Standing up Chastity hugged Shelly tightly. "Will you look after Tink for me?" Shelly asked. "I'm worried about her."

"I will, I promise." Chastity tried to ease Shelly's obvious concern. "Have a good trip and good luck with your new life, Alpha." Chastity hugged her again before releasing her.

"That's not something I ever thought I'd hear." Shelly smiled. "But I'm getting used to it. I'll call and let you know how I'm getting on."

"Good." Chastity nodded before hugging Grant quickly. "Take care, Grant. Hope to see you soon. I've always wanted to visit Scotland."

"I hope to see you at my Pack for a wee holiday, just make sure this big lump here brings you."

Cam shook Shelly's hand. "Bye, and remember what I said 'bout our father. Start out as you mean to go on or he'll walk all over you."

"I'll do my best." Shelly nodded.

Grant looked up at Cam, his eyes a little sad. "I'm sorry we have to leave. I would've preferred to stay a bit longer but I have to get back to the Pack. I've got to introduce my Alpha She-Wolf after all. Take care, mo bhràthair, and please don't be a stranger. Come visit soon."

"I know you have to leave." Cam grabbed Grant in a fierce bear hug. "It was great seeing you, brother, but we both have things we need to take care of now. Good luck and remember to call."

"I will." Grant's voice showing his emotion and sadness at leaving his brother.

"We'll see each other soon." Cam confirmed, patting Grant's back as he turned to take Shelly's hand.

"Are you ready?" he asked as she grinned back at him.

"I sure am, Highlander. Take me home, Grant."

Logan was already outside sitting in the car and waiting patiently as Shelly and Grant got in the back. He rolled the window down, waving to Cam and Chastity standing on the porch. "Bye," Cam said again as the car rolled away, disappearing from sight as it left the Camp.

"Damn, that was harder than I'd thought," Cam admitted, still standing and watching where the car had gone.

"We can visit." Chastity squeezed his hand.

"Yes, we can," Cam agreed as he sighed heavily.

"Are you all set to leave for LA later?" he asked, his eyes still on the road.

"Yes. I'm not taking a lot as you said we'd be going shopping."

"Good." Cam lifted their entwined hands, kissing the top of hers. "I'm going to go visit with Rebecca for a little while. See you in a bit."

"Okay, tell her I'm asking after her and I hope she's feeling better."

"I will," Cam replied as he walked down the stairs.

~ Chapter 8 ~

Rory waved to Cam as he carried on through the Camp. "I'm just going over to the other Pack to catch up with all the gossip from home. If you need me just text but I'll be back before you leave later. You can let me know if there's anything you need me to take care of while you're gone."

Cam stopped walking, shaking his head. "No, it's okay, go and have fun. Rory, I hope you don't mind but I've asked Fergie to take over the Pack while I'm gone."

"I see." Rory closed the distance between them. "I can understand that, Alpha. This was, and should have been, his Pack, if not for the attack on him that is. Things must be a little . . . *strained* . . . between you two now."

"You could say that." Cam's lip raised on one side. "I'm working on a possible solution but I don't want to make any rash decisions. So, Fergie will be in charge while I'm away and I'll meet with him on my return."

"Okay, Cam." Rory grinned cheekily. "Means I'll have more time with Charlie if Fergie's in charge."

"True." Cam smiled back. "Enjoy your time together and you don't need to rush back from your catching up with the guys. I'll see you when I get back." Rory turned to walk away. "Wait," Cam stopped him. "I would appreciate if there are any problems that you phone me. Just a precaution, Rory. I don't want to return to any kind of mess or turmoil of any kind. Okay?"

Rory's demeanor changed, his face serious as he agreed. "Of course. I'll let you know, Cam, you don't need to worry. Fergie may be in charge, but I'll still keep my eyes open for any problems. My allegiance is to the Pack and the Alpha. You, Cam, are Alpha."

"Good." Cam waved him off. "Glad to hear it, now, off you go and don't neglect that lovely mate of yours just because your friends have arrived."

"Oh, no fear of that!" Rory laughed. "She'd come and hunt me down if I tried that."

Cam chuckled as he waved his friend off, turning to continue to go and talk to Rebecca. He was looking forward to it and dreading it in equal parts. She was strong, one of the strongest women he knew, but she was also soft and caring; a side she hid well but one that he was well aware of.

"I hope she's okay." He thought, again and again as he strode through the Camp until he stood in front of the door to the cabin.

Stepping up to it he knocked hard and then waited, hoping that this time, he would gain entrance without any trouble. He had no intention of flying back to LA without personally seeing his friend. No matter what Jacob said.

A K Michaels

The door opened a moment later, Jacob ushering him inside. "She's waiting for you. I'm going for a walk to give you two some privacy. I know you're close to her, Cam, but I won't be far and if you upset her then we *will* have a problem."

"I have no intention of upsetting her." Cam scowled. "You should know me better than that, Jacob."

Jacob shuffled from foot to foot, his face flushing. "I know. I'm sorry, but, fuck, Cam, I can't help but feel overly protective right now. You have to understand that I will do anything, *anything at all*, to ensure she gets better and isn't upset."

Cam stepped up close, placing a hand on Jacob's arm. "I promise I won't hurt her, or upset her. I care for her and I only want to make sure she's okay before I take Chastity to LA."

"Okay, I won't be far." Jacob passed Cam and slowly walked away as Cam closed the door.

"Oh, you're here." Rebecca's voice sounded surprised as he turned around.

"Yes." Cam watched her closely as she walked through from the kitchen. Dressed in a silk, figure hugging dress and a pair of Manolo Blahnik stilettos on her feet. "You look well," Cam said as he closed the distance between them and hugged her close.

"I'm doing better." Rebecca conceded. "It's nice to see you."

"Same here." Cam kept an arm around her shoulders, herding her towards a sofa. "Let's sit and talk."

"If we must." Rebecca frowned.

"We must." Cam confirmed as they sat down. "I need to know you're doing alright and if there's anything I can do to help. A good therapist maybe?"

Rebecca's hand fidgeted with her hemline, tugging it and then smoothing the silk of her dress. "I don't think so."

"Why?" Cam asked. "Look at me, Rebecca, I want to see your face."

She turned towards him, an eyebrow raised and her lip curled up at the side. "What? You think you can see inside me?"

"No, of course not." Cam shook his head. "But I'll certainly be able to tell if you lie to me."

"Why would I lie?"

Cam reached over, taking hold of one of her hands. "Because you are one of the strongest and most stubborn women I know. You don't like anyone to think of you as weak or incapable in any way. So, my friend, we'll talk and you can try and convince me you don't need to go and see a professional."

Rebecca sighed heavily and stared at him. "You are too smart for your own good, Cameron Sinclair. But, as we *are* friends I'll allow it. However, what we say here, stays here.

Understood?"

"Absolutely." Cam agreed. "Now, tell me how you really are."

"It's weird, Cam." Rebecca's hand tried to pull out of his but he held it firmly. "I know that he, you know, *did* things to me. But, I have no memory of it, I was unconscious, so it's kinda hard to get over something that I can't grasp inside my head. I'm also angry, mostly at myself for being so careless that night. If I'd known I was in any kind of danger then he wouldn't have gotten so close to me. I was too wrapped up in helping Fergie, and, well, Jacob. I was so intent on getting back to him that I wasn't even aware of my surroundings. Stupid."

"No, it wasn't stupid." Cam squeezed her hand. "It's not as if any of us were aware that he was a danger."

"That's just it, Cam." Rebecca gave a lopsided half smile. "I should've known. He was a danger when we were going out, a danger when we split up. So I should've realized that when Jacob and I got together that things could potentially go wrong with him. He was more than a little nuts, so I should've at least told Jacob and you that he may cause trouble."

"Hindsight is a wonderful thing, Rebecca. Don't beat yourself up 'bout it."

Rebecca tugged on his hand. "But I do." Her voice rose, anger and upset clear in the shrillness.

"Bridget is dead because of me . . ."

Cam's finger quickly silenced her, reaching up and pressing against her lips. "No. Bridget is dead because she was treacherous and untrustworthy. She betrayed you, Rebecca, in the worst possible way. She couldn't have been so naïve to think that kidnapping you was in any way, shape or form, going to be a good thing. She conspired with Tobias to physically subdue you and take you from Jacob. So I'm sorry if I sound cold, but if she expected things to turn out well then she was just plain stupid."

"I still feel guilty that she's dead," Rebecca whispered, pain in her voice.

"I know you do." Cam put an arm around her shoulders, pulling her close. "But that just shows the kind of person *you* are. You try and hide it real well, but I know you, honey. You've a heart of gold that's so large that it hurts for others. Even when those others don't deserve it."

"Jacob has been rather…over compensating. I can feel his anger and his distress, Cam. I keep telling him I'm okay but I don't think he believes me."

Cam put his head to the side, staring for a moment before answering. "Can you blame him? Rebecca, if this was reversed, if he'd been taken and hurt, tell me, how would you feel?"

Rebecca's answer was immediate.

"Horrified."

"Exactly." Cam hugged her closer. "I think you two are going to be just fine, but it will take time for both of you to heal. Jacob feels responsible in some way, as would I, even if we know that's ridiculous. I just want you to take things slow and if you ever need to talk to someone that's not so close as Jacob is, well, you know I'm here. I also want you to think about talking to a professional. I know that's not your style, that you feel as if you can deal with anything, but this isn't just anything, Rebecca. It's huge, and if you need to, then you just let me know. I'll get you the best damn shrink there is."

"Thank you, Cam." Rebecca smiled. "I'm grateful for the offer and I'll think about it. As I said earlier, it's just kinda hard because I don't remember most of what happened so it's difficult to come to terms with. I do feel much better though so please don't worry. I've spoken with Elijah and he is going to come over when we get home and do a cleansing and healing spell. One for 'my soul' as he puts it."

"That sounds like a good idea." Cam raised an eyebrow. "What's happening with your Witch ceremony thing? Are you going ahead with that or are you putting it off for a while?"

"I want it as soon as possible." Rebecca smirked. "I want Jacob and me to be bound together in both our faiths. Well, not faith, but you know what I mean. We've done his Wolf thing, so I think we need to do my thing. I'll feel more settled once it's done. I hope you and Chastity will come? Stracey has already agreed and I'm hoping we can arrange it within the next two weeks. Elijah is taking over all the arrangements for me and it'll be held at Jacob's place."

"We'll definitely be there. Let me take care of the catering for you. One less thing to worry about. All you need to do is have Elijah give me the date and time and how many guests and I'll do the rest."

Rebecca's eyes suddenly filled with tears and Cam pulled her even tighter. "What's wrong? Did I say something to upset you?"

"No," she sniffed. "I'm just feeling a little fragile. Thank you for the offer, it's not going to be a large affair, but I would love if you could deal with that side of things for me."

"My pleasure." Cam kissed her forehead. "You'll need to tell me if there are any rules or anything regarding the Witchy stuff. I don't want to offend anyone."

Rebecca giggled. "No, no rules, but I'd like it to be simple, in tune with Wicca and the Goddess."

"Okey doke, will do." Cam grinned. "Hell, there are wedding planners for just about anything nowadays, there *must* be one that knows a thing or two about Wicca stuff and I'll make sure to find one."

"I'm sure you will." Rebecca sat up, pulling from his arms. "Now, I gotta go pack. What time are we leaving for LA?"

Cam frowned. "What?" his surprise evident. "Are you going home?"

"Yes." She nodded. "It's time and I want to get back to our place. It's so peaceful and I feel safe there, so, if you don't mind, can we hitch a ride back?"

"Sure." Cam stood. "We'll be leaving after dinner."

"Good. 'Cause Stracey said you're going to a charity shindig so I'm pretty certain that Chastity is going to need my expertise in the clothing department. Hope you plan on spending a lot of money, Cam, 'cause I plan on kitting her out in only the finest outfits I can find."

"You can spend whatever you like though I thought I would take her shopping. I want to be there, see her face when she puts on a gown for the first time."

"Oh, I see. You can come if you don't mind being dragged from shop to shop and absolutely no moaning is allowed. Okay?"

"Sure. Is tomorrow, late morning, say eleven thirty okay for you? We can meet you in town, if that suits?"

"Yes, I'll be there. I'll go in a little earlier and have a look first and then I'll text to tell you where I am."

"Sounds like a plan. Thank you, I'm sure she'll appreciate your input."

"Oh, it won't just be my input. Stracey's coming too. She says she needs a new dress for the ball and she wants to help Chastity pick some clothes as well."

"I see tomorrow is going to be a very expensive one for me."

"Yup, I have my eyes on a new pair of shoes. You can buy them for me as a little treat."

Cam chuckled as he nodded. "I'll be happy to do that."

Rebecca wiped her face, noticing mascara on her fingers. "I gotta go sort myself out. I don't want Jacob thinking you upset me 'cause we both know he'd fly off the handle without even knowing what was what. If you see him outside can you keep him occupied for a few minutes?"

"Yeah," Cam nodded. "I'll do that. See you later and remember, if you need me then all you have to do is call."

"I know, Cam. Thank you. Now shoo, off with you, so I can pretty myself up and get ready to fly home."

Cam laughed as he left the cabin, spying Jacob about a hundred feet away, his eyes glued to the door. "Hey." Cam wandered over, taking his time to help give Rebecca some much needed moments alone. "Rebecca says she's going to pack, she wants to go home. She loves your place and says she feels safe there."

Jacob stared at Cam intently, as if looking for any deceit. "Yeah, she does. She's already said she'll be selling her place. Says mine is far more 'at one' with the Goddess. Whatever the hell that means."

"So long as she's happy then that's all that counts." Cam countered.

"True." Jacob sighed. "How did she seem to you? I know you've known her a hell of a lot longer than me, so, I'd like your opinion."

Cam waited, pondering his answer. "I think she's doing okay. It's as she said to me, she can't remember anything really about what was done to her so she's finding it a little hard accepting that things were done. I don't think she really knows how she feels at the moment. But, Jacob, what I do know is that her love for you is helping. She's desperate to have her Witch thingamabob."

"Handfasting." Jacob's lips twitched. "Strange name, I know, but it's what it's called and she's spoken to Elijah several times about it. Looks like it'll be done sooner rather than later."

"Yeah, she said." Cam looked around the Camp then back at Jacob. "I said I'd take care of the catering for her and I'll be there. Can't wait to see you absolutely tied to that woman. She won't ever let you go, Jacob."

"I know." Jacob's face finally broke into a smile. "I wouldn't want it any other way, Cam."

Cam stepped closer, placing a hand on Jacob's arm. "If you ever need to talk. Even just to vent. Then I'm here. I know it must be hard for you as well as Rebecca. I also know that sometimes we men just need to let off some steam, so, if you need to, just call."

"Thanks." Jacob nodded. "I miss my gym, basically, I'm certain I woulda punched the crap outta it this whole time."

"Yes, I get that." Cam agreed. "If you ever need a sparring partner just let me know."

"Will do." Jacob eyed Cam closely. "You sure she's okay?"

Cam shrugged, his palms held out. "I can't say for sure but she looks as if she's getting there. Time is what's needed. Time and happy memories to take over from bad ones. Give her plenty of happy memories to fill her head so full that it doesn't have space for anything negative. That's what I'd do, my friend."

"Good thinking." Jacob nodded. "I think that's just what I'll do."

"Okay, see you later," Cam said to Jacob's retreating back, his friend already striding back towards Rebecca.

~ Chapter 9 ~

"What?" Rebecca pounced as Cam spun around.

She sat next to Chastity on one of the soft sofas in the jet and he'd thought she was so engrossed that she wouldn't hear him. He'd been wrong. Cam looked to Jacob for some help but the large PI couldn't reply, his emotions were running high and Cam could see it, sense it, and feel it.

"The cat got your tongue?" Rebecca asked, her tone cold. "Or did I just hear you say you were going to go and burn that place down? That's what I heard, right?"

Jacob stood, pacing back and forth within the confines of the cabin as Cam tried to avert a disaster. "You shouldn't eavesdrop, Rebecca, it's not good and usually ends up leading to problems."

"You're sitting less than a few yards from me." Rebecca's face was pure white, anger in every nuance of her body.

"Rebecca. . ." Cam started but stopped when Jacob whirled around.

"Becca, baby, you've got to understand. I can't let that place stand. It has to be destroyed."

She looked between them, her eyes tight and her voice controlled. "No, you two idiots don't understand. You can't just go there and burn it down without me."

Jacob shook his head vigorously. "No, not happening. You're not going anywhere near there. I don't want any bad memories surfacing, Becca, you're doing too well to risk it."

Rebecca stood, her hands on her waist as she glared up at Jacob. "You two don't get it! It's not as simple as that! Tobias was a Witch, a powerful Witch. His essence could still be there and he *could* cause you problems, hurt you even. You are not going there without me and that's final. I'm not arguing about it, with either of you, so don't give me your evil eye, Cam!"

Cam shrugged, looking at Jacob. "Your call, big guy. I've bought the property and we can go and burn it down, or I can get a demolition firm in to destroy it."

Jacob's head shook again. "No, I wish I could let you do that but I can't. I have to watch as it goes up in flames. I *need* to."

Rebecca closed the distance between them, her hand grabbing his shirt in front. "Hey, I understand, I do. After what happened I know you need to put this to rest too. It's harder for you. You saw everything, found Bridget, and me. I have no memories of it so it's like it happened to someone else. But, my big bad Wolf, you are *not* going there without me. At the very least, I want to do a ceremony to have Bridget's soul rest in peace."

Cam flinched. "What? She betrayed you and

you want to help her into the afterlife?"

"Yes." Rebecca didn't look at Cam, keeping her eyes on her mate. "She was misguided, a little spoiled, and used to getting her own way. That doesn't mean she deserved to die, especially not the way she did. So, boys, I'm coming with you and I'll be doing a ritual for her before you torch the place."

"Damn!" Jacob's head fell forwards, their foreheads touching. "Can't I talk you out of it? Please, baby."

"No." Rebecca's voice was firm. "The decision is made and we'll do this together. Okay?"

"I suppose." Jacob relented, his arms going around her to hold her close.

Chastity's voice interrupted them. "Hmm, sorry, I'm not clued up on Witches 'n all that stuff, but, Rebecca, are you saying this guy's ghost is there and can physically hurt them?"

Rebecca turned, nodding. "Afraid so. Most spirits can't harm anyone, scare them a bit maybe, but not hurt them in the physical sense. However, he was very strong in witchcraft and that means he could still be there, and still have some power to wield."

"Hell." Chastity looked over at Cam. "Sorry, but I'm coming too. You're not going there without me, Cam."

"What?" Cam stood, moving quickly to sit beside Chastity. "No, no, and hell no!"

Chastity's jaw stuck out, a very stubborn look in her every nuance. "No is not an option. I'm going and don't you even *dare* try and pull rank on me. You may be Alpha but you're my mate and I will not allow you to go willy nilly into magical danger without me at your side."

Cam sighed, turning to Rebecca for back up. "Tell her she can't go."

"I will not!" Rebecca fumed. "She's as entitled to be there as I am. So long as you all do as I tell you, then we'll be fine."

Chastity pulled Cam's head back around to focus on her. "I am going, Cam. So, why don't we all just agree it's going to be the four of us and decide when?"

Jacob groaned. "Women!"

Rebecca glared at him. "Men!"

"Okay," Cam relented. "Do you want to do this before or after your handfasting thing?"

"Before." Rebecca was quick to answer. "I want this all over with before we have our ceremony."

"Right, well I have some business, the ball, and some other things that need my attention this week." Cam sat back on the sofa, getting comfortable. "What about a week from tomorrow? After that I need to get back to the Pack and decide what I'm going to do about *that*."

"I'm sorry if healing Fergie has put a spanner

104

in the works." Rebecca sat down, pulling Jacob after her. "But, in all good conscience, I couldn't *not* help him. Not when I knew I could, Cam."

"I know." Cam shrugged. "It is what it is. He's my cousin and I'm glad he's healthy and strong again, but it does put my being Alpha of his Pack in a different light."

"Have you thought about what I said?" Chastity asked.

"Yes," Cam replied. "I have, and I'm still mulling it over. I don't ever make rash decisions. I like to think them through and make sure I'm doing what I'm doing for the right reasons. Not just because it's the easiest option."

"I can vouch for that." Jacob chuckled. "If there's ever a person who goes over every available detail, then it's you. But, what is it that Chastity said? Come on, spill."

Cam only smiled. "No, I'm not saying anything just yet."

Rebecca lightened the mood, an evil smile on her face. "So, Chastity, are you all set for our marathon shopping trip tomorrow?"

"I think so." Chastity frowned and bit her lip. "I've no idea about what I'll need though."

"Aww, you don't need to worry." Rebecca grinned cheekily. "I'm an expert and there's nothing I like better than spending Cam's money."

"Yes," Cam groaned. "She certainly does

enjoy that. A little too much in my opinion."

"Aww shush, you've got enough to buy an entire continent, I'm pretty sure you're right on up there with the richest men in the world. So, my friend, I will enjoy kitting Chastity out in a full wardrobe. Formal, casual, and everything in between."

"Surely I don't need all that?" Chastity breathed, a slight waver in her voice.

"Yeah," Cam agreed with Rebecca. "I think you do. I also want stuff for you to take back to the Pack. You lost just about everything when the cabin was blown up. I know you had some stuff that had already been brought over but the majority of your things were blown to hell. So, Rebecca, she needs double of everything apart from formal."

Rebecca rubbed her hands in glee. "Oh goody!"

*****

"I'm kinda nervous," Chastity admitted as Cam pressed the remote control to open the gates to his property.

"Why? It's your home as much as the Pack is now." Cam waited, driving through as soon as there was enough room and clicking the remote again so they closed behind them.

"This is going to sound daft." Chastity's

hand squeezed his thigh. "I mean, I knew you were rich, jeez, we've just flown here on your private jet, but then seeing this car, and the walls around here, it kinda brings it home to me just how much money you have. And," she paused, sighing. "I have nothing."

Cam sped up the long driveway. "You don't have nothing. I've more than enough for both of us. My money is yours too, honey. Don't ever think differently."

"So, you don't want one of those, whatchamacallits . . . a prenup thingie?"

Cam slowed, parking the car outside the front door and turned to her. "Are you crazy? We're Wolves, not humans. We're bonded together, Chastity, we're not getting a divorce, ever. Do you know of any Wolves that have done that? Anyway, as I said, there's more than enough for anything that life throws at us, and then some. So stop worrying about it. Okay? It is not an issue."

Chastity turned to look out the windscreen, her hand flying to cover her mouth. "Oh dear!" she gasped. "This place is huge. Are you telling me only you and Jinx lived here?"

Cam shook his head. "Technically no. I have a woman that lives in a small apartment around by the kitchen. She's human but she's been here for almost as long as Stracey. She cooks, cleans, does errands for me, her name is Kate and she's wonderful. She's like part of my Pack, only she doesn't really understand that. She is aware that Jinx and I are Wolves, although she has never seen us in Wolf form. I hope you like her 'cause she's a huge help and I want you two to get along."

"I see." Chastity's eyes were still taking in the magnificent white house before them. "She won't feel put out with you bringing me here?"

"No." Cam opened his door and got out, coming around to help Chastity. "I've spoken to her and as far as she's aware you're like my wife. Her words, not mine, and she'll treat you like she does me. So, my love, do you want to have a look around?"

"Yes." Chastity took his hand, rising from the sports car and following behind Cam.

"So, this is my home," he said as he ushered her inside. "The lounge is over there, TV room over there, kitchen is through there, turn right and straight on. There's bathrooms all over, I'll show them to you later. Our bedroom is up the stairs and left, straight down to the end, and . . ."

"Stop!" Chastity wailed. "I can't possibly remember all that. Why don't you just walk me through and I'll try and get my bearings."

Cam grinned, his excitement growing at having her here in his home. "Okay, that's probably best. Some of the rooms are only used when I'm throwing a party, usually a charity shindig, so I'll take you straight to the heart of the house."

Chastity held tight to his hand as he led her through several rooms, heading towards the back of the house. He pointed to doors. "Bathroom, my office, Stracey's office and voila." He pushed open a door. "My favorite room."

"Mr. Sinclair!" A homely woman almost squealed. "I saw the gate opening earlier," she pointed to a CCTV screen. "I knew it was you. Welcome home! I have your coffee ready for you."

Cam smiled. "Thank you, Kate. Let me introduce you to Chastity. Chastity, this is Kate."

The woman rushed over, wiping her hands on her apron as she walked. "Hello and welcome. If there's anything you need or I can help with anything at all, just give me a shout."

Chastity shook her hand, looking down at the much smaller woman. "Thank you. I'm a little overwhelmed just now. This place is huge."

"I know what you mean, my dear." Kate turned back towards a coffee machine. "It took me a while to get my bearings. Now, would you like a cup of Mr. Sinclair's favorite coffee? He ships it in from Brazil and I've made your favorite cookies too."

Turning to Cam, Chastity mouthed, "Cookies?" before replying to Kate. "I'd love a cup, thank you."

Cam shrugged. "Who doesn't like cookies, and these here are a legend. Kate's cookies go for high bids you know."

"Bids?" Chastity frowned, obviously having no idea what he meant.

Kate laughed as Cam nodded. "Yes, bids. She very kindly donates boxes of her cookies whenever I do a charity gig here. I tell you, Chastity, they raise a ton of money, everyone wants them and she's even been asked to sell her recipe."

"Oh, I would never do that, not now." Kate's eyes twinkled. "Maybe when I'm about to retire I'll auction it off for my retirement fund."

"No!" Cam's face was a parody of shock. "I'll pay whatever you need when the time comes. These cookies stay here, in my kitchen!"

Chastity smiled at the repartee. "Okay, let me try them out." She reached forward, snatching one from the plate on the counter. As she took a bite she almost moaned with pleasure. "Oh!" was all she managed as Cam burst out laughing.

"Told you." He grinned. "They're the best cookies ever made."

Chastity nodded as she took another bite, Stracey's voice making her jump. "I thought I heard you lot. I assume Chastity's just had her first taste of Kate's cookies?"

"Yes." Cam went over, giving her a hug. "Everything okay? All set for my meeting tomorrow?"

"Yes." Stracey gave a slight frown. "I'm a

little worried about one of the investors though, he's making noises that aren't what I was hoping for."

"Cut him." Cam's tone was sharp. "I don't need anyone else, if needs be I'll do it myself. I have no time to baby anyone and if they're not behind this one hundred percent, then cut them free. If they give you any problems then tell them to contact me direct."

Stracey's grin was on the brink of being evil. "Great! It's that lazy slob, Graham Somers, so I'll take great pleasure in calling him right now and telling him."

Chastity looked between them as she finished her delicious cookie. "What's up?"

"It's a project that Cam's set up, it's a school for kids from the worst parts of the city. He's building it, running it, and paying for everything, including safe transportation for the kids. We've got a big meeting with the City Planning Committee tomorrow to finalize everything and this jackass is only now starting to grumble about his input. It's not even as if he's donating much, tightass."

"Go call him now," Cam ordered. "I don't want any surprises tomorrow. Tell him he's out and if he has a problem I'll deal with him directly. Remind him how much he owes me on that property deal that went bad last year though. That should shut him up pretty damn quick."

Chastity stared wide eyed at Cam and

Stracey as Stracey nodded then strode away. "Wow."

"What?" Cam asked, picking up his own cookie.

"I've never seen this side of you." Chastity moved closer, their bodies almost touching. "High powered businessman. It's kinda hot."

She whispered the last part as Cam stared down at her. "I'm glad you think that and I plan on taking full advantage later, but how about I show you one of my favorite spots in the whole world?"

"Sure," she said, still smirking up at him.

"What time do you want to eat?" Kate asked as Cam opened a set of sliding doors.

"About an hour, if that's okay?" Cam threw over his shoulder.

"That's fine. I'll set up the table for all four of you."

"Okay, now, Chastity, come and have a look outside." Cam led her out onto the back, raised, marble patio which overlooked his large swimming pool and gardens. "That path on the left leads to Stracey's and the one on the other side of the pool leads to the beach. It's private, secure, with no prying eyes. Our nearest neighbor is more than a mile on either side. In fact, more like two that way," Cam pointed left, "and almost three that way." He pointed to the right.

"It's . . . it's," Chastity's breath caught in her throat as she stared out over the pool and down to the sea. "Beautiful doesn't even come close. I'm kinda dumbstruck here, Cam."

"I just want you to be happy here. At ease, I want you to love it just as much as I do."

Chastity looked around again before falling into his arms. "I do. It's beyond anything I've ever seen before, even in magazines! I can't quite believe I'm here, that this is yours."

"No." Cam held her tight. "Not mine, ours. Now, let's go for a walk around the gardens, they're set out so that I can hold parties here and there's plenty of space with seats, lighting, little private areas that are so tranquil that I've hidden there more than once."

"What?" Chastity raised an eyebrow as she stared up at him.

"No!" Cam laughed. "That's not what I meant. When I've been needing some peace, some solitude, I can go and sit and feel as if nothing on earth can touch me. Come, I'll show you my favorite place to sit."

Cam led her down the marble steps, across and past the pool and off to the left, into his immense garden. It took them about ten minutes to reach the spot he wanted to show her, but as soon as they arrived she knew. "This is it," she whispered, taking in the flowers, bushes, and trees that screened the loveseat. "It's like being in the middle of the forest, Cam. You like it so much because it reminds you of that. Of being Wolf."

"Pardon?" Cam said, looking around them and sitting down. His eyes then saw things as she did and his heart sped up. "You're right. I'd denied my beast for so long that I didn't even realize."

"I love it here." Chastity sat beside him, her head on his shoulder. "When we're not back at the Pack then I think I'll be spending a lot of time here. Is it safe to morph?"

Cam nodded. "Of course. The gardeners only come twice a week, Monday's and Thursday's, unless I've got some event planned and then they come and make sure everything's all tidy and prettied up. But they only work during the day, they leave at five o'clock sharp, so any evening is safe to change if you want to."

"Oh, yes, I'll definitely be going Wolf and roaming around here."

"I might even join you, though that will be a first for me." Cam pulled her closer, his chin on her head as they relaxed.

"I'd like that." Chastity's hand moved over to clasp his shirt. "Our Wolves will be happy here, Cam. I know it."

"I'm glad you like it here." Cam's hand covered hers. "I was nervous you wouldn't feel at home and that's what it is, baby, our home. Or one of them."

"Yes, we have two," Chastity agreed.

"No," Cam chuckled. "We have much more than that. I have houses kinda all over, here in the US, Europe, Asia, Mexico, I've even got a beach house in Australia that I love. The swimming there is phenomenal, you'll love it."

"Oh, I see." Chastity shook her head. "Well, I don't, not really. Having anything other than a cabin on Pack land is new to me. I guess I'll need to get used to it."

"You will." Cam's tone was firm, no nonsense. "You'll take to it like a duck to water, I just know it. You may have been raised only within a Pack, but, you are full of elegance, poise and charm that can never be bought and paid for. It comes from within, honey, and you have it in spades."

"I hope so, I really don't want to make a fool of myself tomorrow, or you."

"You most definitely won't do that." Cam insisted. "Trust me, you'll be fine. There are some snooty people about, but I rarely give them the time of day. I hate when someone thinks that money alone entitles them to anything, especially the ones who expect others to kowtow to them. I usually shoot 'em down in flames pretty quick. If I don't, then Stracey certainly does. She's got a feisty mouth on her at times."

"I know." Chastity grinned. "I've heard her and I think I'll be keeping her close to me at the ball tomorrow. For back up."

Cam sniggered, his eyes twinkling. "You'll have back up times three, me, Jinx and Stracey, so don't worry."

"I'll try."

"I think we should head back. I was going to show you our room before dinner but we've been here a while so it'll have to wait."

"Okay, but I'm a little tired. Can we have an early night? I get the feeling I'm going to need my energy for tomorrow. Rebecca's got big plans for shopping."

Standing up, Cam pulled her to her feet. "Sure, and yeah, I know. She's got her eyes on some new shoes that I'm going to be paying for, but, Rebecca being Rebecca, you can bet she'll want the damn purse to go with it."

"Probably," Chastity agreed as they meandered back through the gardens for dinner.

A K Michaels

~ Chapter 10 ~

Jinx and Stracey joined them and they chatted easily throughout the meal. Chastity moaned in pleasure several times as she tasted the food. "This is glorious," she finally said as she finished.

"Aye," Jinx agreed heartily. "Miss K is a fabulous cook."

"Miss K?" Chastity asked, looking between Jinx and Cam.

"Our nickname for her." Cam smiled. "We're lucky to have her and I dread to think what we'll do when the time comes for her to retire."

"Don't even say that." Jinx scowled. "I hate to think that there'll be a day when she's not here."

"I know." Cam nodded. "But, we have to face it at some point. She is human after all."

"I try not to think about it." Jinx admitted.

"Maybe Kate can teach me how to cook some of her dishes?" Chastity asked, before sipping her wine.

"That's a good idea." Cam grinned. "We can ask her tomorrow. I told her to finish up and go rest, but, knowing Miss K, she'll be sitting with a book in her hands. She loves to read and I'm going to get her one of those new ereaders. I've seen her wince a couple of times when holding a book but she'll never admit her joints are hurting her. I think a light reader for her to use would help."

117

"That's a great idea." Stracey agreed. "Then I can buy her a ton of stuff for it, and give her a gift certificate so she can buy what she wants."

"Good thinking, Stracey." Chastity turned to Cam. "I might ask my Wolf here if I can get one. I've always wanted one."

"Of course." Cam reached over, his fingers lacing with hers. "Is there anything else you want? Just ask, baby, and it's yours. Have you looked at the different ones available? Do you know what one you want, or shall I have a look and get you what I think's best?"

"Oh . . ." Chastity looked thoughtful for a brief moment. "I think you should decide. I don't have any real knowledge about them so I trust you to pick it."

"Do you read a lot?" Stracey asked, sipping her water.

"Anything I can get my hands on. I was pretty limited, you know, before, but I've read some of the books that Angel and Marie had. I've come across a few new authors that I'd like to get the rest of their stuff." Chastity laughed. "Now, I know you'll think this funny, but I've recently finished one by Monica La Porta, she writes about Immortals, and even has Wolves in her stories. I know it's weird reading 'bout that stuff, but I loved them. I'd love to get the rest in her series."

"Wolves huh?" Jinx grinned. "Do they howl

118

at the moon and get hunted down by humans?"

"No," Chastity stated. "They're not that far removed from us, but hers can't change at will and humans don't know about them, or any of the other species. They're set in Rome—she's from Italy—and the way she writes makes me feel as if I'm there and seeing everything for myself."

"Rome?" Cam cocked his head to the side. "I think I can arrange that."

"Arrange what?" Chastity asked, confused.

"A visit to Rome. I'll take you and you can see all these places you've read about for yourself." Cam squeezed her hand. "Would you like that?"

Chastity's eyes were like saucers as she nodded. "Yes. I've never been out of the US and only been to a few states here. Rome, you really mean it? Oh, I'll need a passport, won't I? I don't have paperwork to get one!"

"Yes, I mean it and don't worry. I'll get one of my lawyers to sort out the paperwork." Cam shrugged. "It may take a little while so why don't we plan it for a few months from now? That way you can read all of this . . . what's her name?"

"Monica La Porta."

"Yes, you can read all of her books and if you write down the places you want to see I can arrange it. Okay?"

Chastity nodded but she appeared to have lost her voice.

Jinx smirked. "Okay, a word of warning, Chastity. I get the feeling that anything that you express even the smallest interest in is gonna be bought. Am I right, Cam?"

"Aye." Cam's eyes twinkled. "I'd buy her the whole damn world if I could."

Cam stared at Chastity and saw the telltale glisten of tears, one breaking free and rolling down her cheek. His finger quickly wiped it away as he moved closer, worry in his voice. "What's wrong? Have I upset you?"

"No," Chastity struggled to speak. "I'm happy."

Stracey chuckled. "Okay, Jinx, this is about the time we make a quick exit. I have a feeling things are going to get intense now. See ya in the morning."

Stracey was up and pulling Jinx after her. "Goodnight." Jinx threw over his shoulder as Stracey dragged him out.

"Happy tears?" Cam asked tenderly.

"Yeah," Chastity sniffed. "I'm not used to this. Having someone look out for me, buy stuff for me. It's a little hard getting used to it."

"I'll move mountains to make you happy, baby." Cam stroked her face. "Why don't we go upstairs and I'll show you our room."

"Sounds good." Chastity smiled, rising and holding out her hand.

Cam took hold of it and stood. "If you want

to change anything just let me know."

"Change? Like what?" she asked as they left the dining room, walking along the hallway towards the stairs.

"Anything, but especially our bedroom." Cam smirked. "It's set up for me so it may not be to your taste."

"Aah, okay." Chastity followed him up the large staircase. "I need to see it first but I'm trying to imagine how it'll look."

"I don't think it'll be what you're thinking, but, we'll see." Cam tugged her down the corridor towards a set of double doors.

"You surprise me a lot, Cam," Chastity admitted. "You're tough, and soft, you're a hard-nosed businessman, and a caring Alpha. You're just full of contradictions."

Cam pushed one of the doors open and waved her inside, following behind. Chastity stopped a few feet inside the extremely large space, her eyes flitting all around before she turned back to him. "You've done it again," she said, her arm moving all around to take in the room. "It's most definitely not what I expected. It's beautiful."

She continued to stare at the room. "Masculine but with soft touches. I really like the neutral color with the dash of green. It's welcoming but not too fussy. Classy but not stuffy and that bed is amazing! Where did you get it and how old is it?

It looks like an antique."

"It is." Cam grinned. "Well, apart from the mattress, that's new, but the bed is over two hundred years old."

Chastity walked over, running her fingers over the ornate carvings on one of the four posts. "It's gorgeous."

"Anything you'd change?" Cam asked as he slid up behind her, his arms circling her waist.

"Hmm, maybe just the drapes. Something brighter would be nice, and bedding to match."

Cam swept her long hair out of the way before gently kissing the back of her neck. "Done."

"You're too easy." Chastity laughed as his hands slipped under her top, his fingers softly roaming upwards.

"Aye." Cam chuckled, turning her around to kiss her lips. "You can have anything you want, my mate, anything."

Chastity reached up, her fingers tracing his lips. "I don't want a lot, Cam. I just want us to be happy and have a long life together. I've learned the hard way just how lucky I am to have found you. So, my Alpha, how about we try out our new marital bed?"

"That's just what was running through my head too." Cam picked her up, easily carrying her to the side of the bed. "I hope you're not too tired, baby, 'cause I'm feeling rather adventurous tonight."

"Really?" Chastity asked, breathlessly. "Hmm, I think I can accommodate you, that's if you can keep up with me."

Cam laughed, depositing her on the bed and starting to undress. "Better get those clothes off, or better still, leave them, I want to rip them from your body."

"What? And just how do you plan on doing that?"

As he dropped his clothing to the floor Cam raised an eyebrow, before focusing his power to allow his claws to extend from his fingers. "With these," he said as he knelt on the bed beside her.

"Oh." She gasped as his claws expertly ripped her clothing to shreds.

"There." Cam grinned. "That's much better."

"Just as well we're going shopping tomorrow 'cause those were my last pair of decent jeans." Chastity giggled as he pulled her up, his mouth covering hers hungrily.

"I'll buy you more." Cam nuzzled her neck. "Dozens and dozens of jeans, as many as you want."

"All I want right now is you. Cam, make me come, have me screaming your name as you roar mine."

"I will, baby, I will." Cam lowered them back to the bed then turned her onto her belly. "All fours," he instructed her, moving her slightly to position her the way he wanted. "Good, that's it."

Chastity's groan of pleasure as he entered her caused his heart to speed up. His strong thighs straining to control his thrusts as his hands held her hips. "By the Goddess, you are the most beautiful woman I've ever seen. You look so damn sexy tonight, Chastity."

Looking over her shoulder, her eyes hooded and full of desire. "Faster," she breathed.

"No." Cam shook his head.

"Yes!" She implored, moving herself back onto him.

"It'll be over too quick." He tried to contain himself when all he really wanted to do was pound into her as quickly as he could.

"I know." She gasped, her body quivering beneath his touch.

Cam's breathing increased, his heart pounding rapidly as he acquiesced. His hips moved quicker, thrusting with abandon as Chastity's vocalization grew louder and louder. "Yes!" she screamed, over and over, until he felt her orgasm start deep within her as her sheath tightened, then spasmed all around him.

As she cried out his name, his hands tightened their grip, holding her steady as he drove his cock deep inside her, faster and harder than ever. His head fell back as he roared her name with abandon, his release shooting from him as his entire being filled with ecstasy. His Wolf reared itself from the recesses of his mind, causing his canines to erupt from his gums, and he fell forward, over her back and sank them into her shoulder.

As her blood fell over his tongue, another set of feelings exploded inside him. Love, happiness, tenderness and devotion, ran rampant through him. "Mine!" he exclaimed as he tugged his razor sharp teeth from her skin.

"Yes," she answered his claim as they both fell forward onto the bed in a tangled heap.

Some moments later, once both of them had recovered, Cam pulled her into his arms. "I love you."

"I love you too." Chastity looked up at him. "I think we should shower and get some rest. I've got this shopping stuff tomorrow and then we're going to my very first ball. I think I'm going to need all the sleep I can get tonight."

"Aww," Cam tried to look upset. "I thought we were going to be giving this bed a good long try out."

"Tomorrow night." Chastity frowned. "That's if I survive the evening."

"I've told you, don't worry, it'll be fun." Cam shrugged. "Okay, maybe not fun, but it most definitely won't be as bad as you're thinking it'll be."

"So you say." Chastity sat up. "Come on, where's the bathroom?"

Cam pouted. "Over there, door in the corner."

"Stop that." Chastity shook a finger at him. "You're acting like a schoolboy who's got his first girlfriend and can't get enough of her."

"I can't." Cam protested as he got out of the bed to follow her. "I want you all the time. It's kinda like an addiction. Oh wait, 'My name is Cameron Sinclair and I'm addicted to having sex with Chastity,' how does that sound?"

"Ridiculous." Chastity shook her head as she opened the bathroom door.

Cam bumped into her as he trailed behind. "What's wrong?"

Chastity stood with eyes wide and then turned to look over her shoulder. "This is your bathroom? Shit! It's huge and I'm not even sure I know what some of this stuff is. Is *that* a shower? If so, how the hell do you use it? It's got more buttons and dials than the cockpit of your jet!"

"Yes," Cam smiled. "That's the shower and I'll show you how to use it. That's a Jacuzzi bath," he pointed to the overly large bath at the back of the room. "The rest of the stuff is just normal bathroom stuff. If there's anything you're not sure how to use then all you have to do is ask."

"Dang!" Chastity's fingers ran over the Italian marble that housed two sinks. "These are about as big as the baby baths we use for cubs." She

126

moved on to an inset cupboard, a crystal handle the only clue that anything was there. "Hairdryer? Do you use a hairdryer?"

Cam nodded. "Occasionally, if I'm in a hurry for a meeting. But if you look below that you'll see my shaving gear is in there and below that on the shelf are some fresh towels. Those are only small ones, the big bath towels are in the next cupboard along. There should also be a supply of toiletries there for you. I got Kate to pick some stuff up for you but if they're not to your liking then write down what it is you want and she'll get them."

"Jeez, this is like nothing I could ever imagine a bathroom to look like." She ran her hands over the edge of the shower stall.

"It's also a sauna, do you like those?"

Chastity shook her head. "I've no idea, never used one."

"Well, we can spend an evening in here and try everything out, that's if you'd like to?" Cam's fingers trailed down her back.

"Yes, I think I might, but for now I just want an honest to goodness, ordinary shower. So, can you show me how to work this thing?"

Laughing he opened the door. "Sure." He pointed to a couple of the numerous dials. "Here to turn water on and temperature, and here for how you want the water. Overhead, jets all over, waterfall, or just plain old shower."

"Plain old shower, please."

Cam turned the shower on, water pouring down. "Okay, here you go. But, I sincerely hope you're letting me shower with you?"

"Of course." Chastity chuckled. "Wouldn't be as much fun on my own."

"No," Cam's voice came out low and husky. "It wouldn't."

"Oh, I know that tone." Giggling she took hold of his hand, pulling Cam into the large enclosure after her.

"Good." Was all Cam replied before pulling her back into his arms. "Let's test this out, I've never had sex here before."

"Really?" Chasity asked, shock clear in her voice.

"Yes, really." Cam kissed her softly before pulling back to stare into her eyes. "I didn't bring women to my home. So, my white Wolf, I've never had sex here, in our bed, or anywhere else within this house."

"That's a surprise." Chastity quivered beneath his touch. "With your reputation I'da thought you'd had sex just 'bout everywhere."

"Nope." Cam disagreed. "Never here. Not even once."

"I'm glad." Chastity nuzzled his nipple, causing him to groan loudly. "I want to make everywhere 'ours' and only ours."

128

"We will, baby." Cam lifted her, bracing her back against the stall. "I promise," he whispered as his hardness pressed inside of her once again.

~ Chapter 11 ~

"Oh my good grief!" Chastity exhaled loudly as she sat down on the bottom stair. "Who would've thought shopping could be so tiring. I'm all shopped out!"

Cam laughed, his arms full of brightly wrapped boxes, his fingers holding a myriad of bags. "I'm just glad Rebecca and Stracey finally let us go! I thought they were going to keep us for at least another hour."

"I know!" Chastity's stomach rumbled loudly. "And we didn't even get a chance to eat lunch. I'm starved."

"Why don't you go and see what Kate's got. She's always got something going on and I'll take all these up to our room."

"Okay." Chastity pushed herself up. "Don't be long though."

"I won't." Cam strode up the stairs, feeling with his feet as his sight was impaired by the shopping bags. A large smile on his face as he thought of the moment he first saw Chastity in an evening gown. The soft material skimming over her curves as the Swarovski crystals at the neckline shimmered and sparkled as she did a twirl for him. Chastity giggled as Rebecca and Stracey stood to the side.

"That's the one for this evening." Rebecca

nodded, her arms crossed and a no-nonsense look on her face.

Cam hadn't argued as the gown was so exquisite and Chastity had looked beyond beautiful. She was a vision of elegance and he couldn't wait to show her off later. He knew every single male's eyes would follow her and he knew he'd have to keep his beast reigned in tight, so as not to make a scene.

The shoes that Stracey had produced with a grinning "Voila!" set off the dress perfectly and Chastity didn't wobble once as she paraded back and forth. He'd felt so . . . proud . . . yes that was the feeling he'd felt as she walked with poise, her back straight, her head high, and a huge smile on her face. Boy, he couldn't wait to show her the entire world, especially Rome, the place she'd read so much about in the books she loved. He thought he might find out the details for the author, what was her name? Monica something . . . yes, Monica La Porta, he'd get Stracey to find out about her and send a bunch of roses to thank her for making Chastity happy.

He'd do anything to make her happy.

Kicking their door open he managed not to drop anything and lay everything onto the bed. Cam rummaged through the bags until he found the ones with the garments for the evening's ball. He carefully laid out the shoes and lingerie before hanging up the gown, he didn't want it to get wrinkled, and then he chuckled at the packages covering the bed. "That's not even half of them," he said to himself, shaking his head and leaving the room to go and find Chastity.

He followed the noise of chatter coming from the kitchen, finding Chastity and Kate talking like two old friends. Kate was whirling around the kitchen, talking and laughing, as well as putting a meal together, as Chastity sipped a bottle of water.

"I see you two are getting on," Cam said as he stood behind Chastity, his arms circling her waist.

"I was just telling Kate about our shopping trip." Chastity leaned back into his body as she looked over her shoulder at him.

The sight brought the memory of the previous night stampeding to the forefront of his brain and he couldn't stop his reaction; his manhood now rock hard and pressing into Chastity. She raised an eyebrow at him as he shrugged, whispering, "Sorry, last night just popped into my head."

"You are so naughty," she whispered back, her eyes flitting to Kate then back again.

"What are you two lovebirds whispering about?" Kate walked over, placing two plates of food down on the breakfast bar.

"Nothing." They both replied before bursting out laughing.

"Hmm." Kate smiled. "I suspect it was something private, so I won't pry. Now, eat up, Chastity says you missed lunch and you know you'll only get those tiny snack things at the ball later."

"I know," Cam grumbled. "I hate the ones where it's waiters walking around with trays of those tiny hors d'oeuvres, you'd need to eat a full tray or two to fill you up. At least this one starts a bit later so it's over quicker."

Chastity frowned as she sat on one of the tall stools and pulled her plate closer. "I thought you said we'd have fun? You sound as if it's anything but fun."

"We will." Cam popped some hot chicken into his mouth, humming with pleasure at the taste. "I would rather be home here, with you, and not with a couple of hundred strangers. Well, not all are strangers but a lot are."

"Stracey is definitely coming, isn't she?" Chastity sounded worried as she stared at Cam.

"Yes." Cam reassured her. "I promise. She says she'll stick by your side the whole evening, just to make sure you're okay. Don't worry, baby."

"What's it for? The ball, is it for anything I'd know about?"

Cam shrugged as he picked up his drink that Kate had just deposited in front of him. "It's for a homeless shelter in the city. This one is a little different because it only caters to kids under the age of twenty one. They are the most vulnerable out there and we're trying to enlarge it and get a couple more social workers on board. Ones that specialize in kids with problems."

"That's a great thing, for the kids I mean, it must be so hard for human children to be on the streets of a big city." Chastity bit her lower lip briefly. "Do any of ours turn up on the streets?"

"Sometimes." Cam liked the way her mind immediately transferred to their own kind. "Although they don't tend to broadcast what they are, but, Jinx and I make regular rounds of the kids when we're here. We can pick any Wolves out and then we do our best to help them get into another Pack. If they're on the streets, there's usually a damn good reason for it and they don't want to return to their home. But, most of them will go to another Pack, so long as they can visit and check it out first. But there are still some that are wary of joining a Pack again, and I'm still trying to come up with a solution to that."

Chastity looked thoughtful as she ate, almost finishing before she turned back to Cam. "What about a kind of orphanage, one for young Wolves who have nowhere to go, for whatever reason? We could have it on our land, near the Pack camp but not in it. Some cabins and things for the kids to keep them occupied. Or . . ." Chastity's face grew animated as she bounced on her seat. "What about some of the adult Wolves mentoring the kids. Teaching them to hunt, about herbs for healing, survival, stuff like that."

Cam stared at her face, saw the twinkle of excitement in her eyes. "That's a good idea. Let me think on it but I think it could work. It could also be a halfway stage for the kids. For the ones that haven't decided to trust a Pack again yet. They would have somewhere safe to stay while they readjust and learn that not all Packs are harsh and cruel."

"Yes, exactly." Chastity nodded vigorously.

"I can bake you a ton of cookies." Kate smirked. "Once they taste them they'll want to stay."

Cam laughed. "They sure will."

"Okay, Cam, you think it through and then we can talk about it again." Chastity slid from her stool. "Now, I'm going for a long, relaxing bath, and then I'll get ready for the ball. You, Mr. Sinclair, stay out of the room. I want you to wait and see me when I've got everything on, my hair done, and shock 'n horror, my make-up done."

"What?" Cam almost stuttered. "You don't want me to come join you?"

Kate sniggered as she removed the plates, Chastity shaking her head. "Nope. Come and get what you need and get ready in another room. It's not as if there's not a ton of 'em for you to use. I'll meet you at the bottom of the stairs when it's time for us to leave. Okay?"

Cam scowled. "I suppose." He grumbled as he stood. "I'll go and get my things now. I won't be far, in the next room, so if you need me just shout."

Chastity pulled his head down, kissing him gently. "Thank you. I want to see your face when you see me, my Alpha."

"I know." Cam nibbled her bottom lip. "But I woulda rather have joined you in the tub."

"Yes," Chastity replied with a grin. "I know that but then it would mean I'da been rushing to get ready and I want to take my time. Stracey said she'll come over and help me with my hair."

"Okay, baby." Cam turned and walked away, his shoulders slumped in mock despair.

"Kate, when Stracey arrives can you tell her to come on up?" Chastity followed Cam slowly, wanting to give him time to get his things before she got there.

"I surely will and if there's anything else you need just let me know."

"I will, thank you, Kate." Chastity turned around, quickly grabbing a cookie from the counter and nibbling on it.

Kate waved her off. "Go, relax for a little before you need to get ready and I'll send Stracey up as soon as she gets here."

"Thanks," Chastity said again as she left the kitchen.

As Chastity entered the bedroom Cam already had his things in his arms. "I'm going to do some work before I need to get ready. I'll see you downstairs later, okay?"

"Yes." Chastity looked serious. "Don't work too hard though. I don't want you all tired out before the evening's even started."

"Oh, I won't be too tired, for anything the night brings, baby." Cam wiggled his eyebrows. "If you get my meaning?"

"I do." She laughed, slapping him on the butt. "Now scoot. I want to try out that big Jacuzzi thingie and think about what I want my hair to look like. I want it different to anything you've seen before."

"You'll look gorgeous no matter what you do." Cam stopped at the door. "You absolutely sure you don't want me to join you in the bathroom?"

Chastity smiled up at him. "Tomorrow we can bathe together but right now I need to unwind. I didn't realize how much that shopping trip stressed me out. I'm not comfortable not looking at price tags and I'm sure I'd have a heart attack if I knew how much all this stuff cost. Plus, I need to put everything away." Her arm swept over the mound of packages on the bed.

"Okay, but I'll hold you to that." Cam stepped out into the hall. "Tomorrow we'll share a bottle of champagne and strawberries while we're in the Jacuzzi."

"I look forward to it." Chastity closed the door, turned and looked at the pile on the bed. "Damn, I better get started," she said to herself as

137

she went over.

Cam heard her as she rushed around the bedroom, listening for a few moments before taking his things to the bedroom next door. Afterwards he made his way to his office, some plans in his head that he wanted to check out. Chastity's idea had his mind working overtime in order to make it happen. It was already a good idea but with some improvements it would be even better and he knew just the spot he wanted to build on.

He called Jinx, filling him in on the idea for the project, and then put him to work on a cost estimate. "If you can have some provisional numbers for me this evening I'd really appreciate that. I'd like to surprise Chastity later."

"Okay, Sin," Jinx slipped back to using the nickname he'd fashioned for Cam. "I'll also let Stracey know, she can look into if we'll need any planning permits and stuff like that. Though, with it being on Pack land, I would think it would be okay but better to make sure."

"Yes." Cam's voice firm and businesslike. "Everything needs to be above board and legal. I don't want anything getting in the way and postponing things. If we get our asses in gear we can have this up and running pretty fast. There's another load of boys coming from home next week and there's also others coming to join Wild Flower, so we'll have all the labor we'll need. I want this done as quickly as possible, Jinx."

"Okay, I'm on it." Jinx hung up without a goodbye.

Cam smiled, it meant his Beta was caught up with the project too. He'd be just as excited as Chastity on this, Jinx was a sucker when it came to kids in need, and if it were Wolf youngsters then he'd be doubly so. As he pondered on that he also thought of Chastity's proposal for the solution to the Fergie situation. With this new venture for the kids it looked as if her solution would work even better. Although he'd have to change a few things around but, hey, he was Alpha, he could change things if he wanted.

As time ticked past, he almost lost track and ended up rushing upstairs for a quick shower before dressing in one of his hand-made tuxedos, white shirt and bow tie. Fastening the laces of his Italian leather dress shoes, he stood in front of the mirror, checking his bow was straight, before splashing on just a hint of aftershave. When he walked past his bedroom door he heard Stracey and Chastity giggling like schoolgirls.

Then he heard Chastity's voice. "No! He didn't!"

Stracey's reply was immediate. "He did! You should've seen everyone's faces. It was hilarious. I don't think I've enjoyed one of those boring meetings as much as I did that one. I thought Somers was gonna have a coronary right there in the conference room."

Cam smirked, remembering the meeting Stracey was talking about. The one where he'd told Graham Somers to get off his ass and leave the meeting immediately. He'd told him in no uncertain terms that he didn't have time to deal with fools, no matter how much they were bringing to the table.

He'd enjoyed getting that particular moron off that deal and enjoyed it even more the previous day when he'd told Stracey to cut him from the school project. In fact, he had plans to blackball the man completely. He'd let Stracey know this evening that if Somers' name came up in anything Cam was proposing that she was to let him know, so he could rid himself of the man once and for all.

The man was the kind that Cam loathed, born into money and feeling it entitled him in some way. Not as far as Cam was concerned and he hoped Somers wasn't at the ball, the last thing he wanted was Chastity meeting the narrow minded, entitled thinking ass, and obnoxious to boot.

Cam pushed thoughts of Somers from his mind, pacing back and forth before the staircase, checking his watch and waiting, rather impatiently, for his mate. His hearing picked up the sound of a door opening, heels clicking on the hardwood floor of the hallway as his eyes locked upwards to where he'd get his first glimpse of the women.

He heard Chastity whisper frantically, "Are

you sure I look okay? I'm not sure about the make-up, I don't usually wear such a bright color on my lips."

Stracey's response was immediate and firm. "You look lovely. Stop worrying, and the lipstick sets everything else off to a tee. Now, deep breath and go and let him see you. I know he'll be down there holding his breath so go and put him out of his misery."

Cam smirked as he heard his love's footsteps speed up and finally he caught a glimpse as she came into view. His heart stuttered, his breathing stopped, and his eyes blinked several times at the vision before him. Chastity stood at the top of the stairs, one hand on the bannister and one holding the bead encrusted small purse that matched her gown.

As she started to descend the stairs, his eyes raked every single inch of her, her beauty shining so bright he was sure she'd light up an entire room. Her gorgeous blonde locks were a mix of curls and waves, with some of it pinned up with a few tendrils framing her perfect face and some falling down her bare back. The dress she wore was an almost exact match to his eyes, the blue complimenting her coloring beautifully. The low back meant he could feel her skin under his fingers all night long without raising any eyebrows, and he planned on doing just that.

His hand sneaked into his pocket, fingering

the gift he had for her. One that had taken quite a few surreptitious calls to get. Cam hoped she liked it and the meaning behind it. Her shy smile as she started to walk down the stairs caused his breath to catch again, her gown flowing behind her as she elegantly made her way towards him.

"You look absolutely divine." He grinned boyishly up at her. "Everyone is going to be jealous you're on my arm tonight, baby."

"Shush." Chastity giggled as she took the last step to finally stand before him.

Cam leaned forward gently kissing her cheek. "I don't want to mess up your lips, the color suits you." He commented on the lush ruby red covering her mouth. "I have something for you."

He removed his hand from his pocket and held the small box in front of him, opening it to reveal a simple diamond solitaire ring. "Now, before you say anything, this is from my heart, Chastity. I know we've been bonded, but we also live in the human world and I want everyone to understand exactly what you mean to me. So, my love, would you do me the honor of becoming my legal wife?"

Cam heard Stracey laugh as Chastity gasped, her hand flying to cover her mouth, soft tears glistening in her eyes. His finger rose, wiping a stray one away. "Hey, don't cry."

Stracey prodded her back. "No, don't you dare cry. I spent ages doing that make-up. And for goodness sake answer him before he falls at your feet pleading."

Cam threw Stracey a withering look before focusing on Chastity again. Her smile lit up her face as she nodded. "I'll take that as a yes?"

"Yes!" She almost screamed, throwing her arms around his neck.

"Good!" Cam disentangled them, taking the ring and placing it on her finger. "'Cause I wasn't leaving this house until you agreed."

"It's perfect, and it fits. How did you know my size?"

Cam smirked. "I'm pretty good at guessing what size a woman is for jewelry, kind of a habit I grew over the years. Now I'm glad I only need to pick for you, my mate, or, I should say my fiancé."

"What the hell have I missed?" Jinx's surprised voice interrupted them.

Stracey went over to her mate, linking her arm through his. "Only our Sin's marriage proposal, with ring included! Boy, Cameron Sinclair, you are gonna break some hearts tonight!"

"Damn!" Jinx went over, punching Cam's shoulder. "You didn't tell me you were going to do this. Congratulations, both of you!"

"It was a surprise." Cam laughed at Jinx's scowl. "I don't tell you *everything*, Jinx. Now Chastity needs to decide on what she wants to do regarding a formal wedding ceremony. Any thoughts?"

Chastity looked terrified, looking up at Cam with eyes as wide as saucers. "Nothing big. I mean it, Cam. I know you're a high flyer in the human world but I'm not looking for anything fancy. I'll think about it and let you know."

"Whatever, wherever, and whenever you want, baby. It's totally up to you."

"Good." Chastity let out a long breath. "This is such a good day, one of the best I've ever had. Now, shouldn't we be on our way?"

Cam checked his watch. "Yes, let's go folks."

Chastity took his offered arm as he led them outside to a waiting limo, her eyes flitting to him as he helped her in. "A limo ride, never had one of those."

"Get used to it." Stracey smiled. "It's the way he always arrives at events."

"Must cost a fortune." Chastity let slip before blushing.

"I own the company." Cam grinned as he told the driver to go and gave him instructions for picking them up.

"He owns the company?" Chastity asked, looking at Stracey.

"Sure." Stracey nodded. "Just one of possibly hundreds he owns. Cam has a very diverse portfolio of businesses he owns, some outright and some as a partner. Though he does prefer owning something completely, saves on any arguments in the boardroom."

"He's got his fingers in a lot of pies, varied and plentiful, and he likes to be in control. Don't ya?" Stracey grinned over at Cam.

"I do." He agreed. "Now, can we start to celebrate? After all, I've just become engaged."

He reached over and opened the fridge, pulling an already chilled bottle of champagne out and popping the cork. Jinx passed out flutes and Cam filled them up. "Here's to the most beautiful fiancée in the entire universe."

Chastity raised her glass to her lips, taking a small sip. "Here's to the man that makes me the happiest woman alive."

Cam sipped his as Jinx and Stracey looked on. Stracey sighed. "Shoot!" she exclaimed, causing Cam and Chastity to turn and stare.

"What?" Chastity asked, worriedly. "Is something wrong?"

"No," Stracey sighed. "I can see tonight's festivities will be ending sooner rather than later though. You two will be desperate to get home just about as soon as we arrive."

Jinx laughed. "I think you're right."

Stracey poked him hard in the ribs. "Hey, I'm always right."

Cam grinned, pouring some more

champagne for them all. "Hey, I have to stay just long enough for etiquette's sake, then we'll be leaving. My *fiancée* and I have a date with a Jacuzzi, champagne and strawberries."

~ Chapter 12 ~

Cam could feel her nerves, her hand shaking in his as they entered the ball. "It's okay, baby, no need to be nervous."

Chastity looked up at him. "Sorry, I just don't want to make a fool of myself. What if I don't know what to say to people? I'm not used to being around this many humans, Cam."

Stracey moved up closer to them, walking at Chastity's side with Jinx on her other arm. "Hey, deep breath, Chastity. Don't panic, honey, you're on the arm of the richest, most powerful man here. Trust me when I say nobody is going to do anything to upset you."

At that very moment a young, tall, buxom blonde arrived in front of them, her eyes raking over Chastity. "Cameron, so nice of you to come."

"Brenda." Cam inclined his head, apparently ignoring the outstretched hand of the woman. "I'd like to introduce you to my fiancée, Chastity. Chastity this is Brenda, she helps out with the catering for these charity shindigs."

Everyone saw the steely, cold glint enter the woman's eyes as she stared at Cam a moment or two too long, before turning to gaze at Chastity. "Your fiancée? I didn't know you were seeing anyone, Cam."

Chastity held her hand out and this time it

147

was the woman who ignored the gesture. "Hello," Chastity said, her beast rampaging around in her head at the way this female was encroaching on her mate.

Brenda turned, giving Chastity a withering glare. "When did this happen?"

Cam's tone was ice cold as he glowered at the woman. "None of your business, Brenda. Now, I'll forgive your momentary rudeness, this time only. However, act like that toward my fiancée again and you will never work another ball. I'll make damn sure of it."

Chastity's back straightened and she held her hand out again. "I said, hello." Her voice was strong, firm and pure Alpha female.

Brenda blinked, first at Cam then at Chastity, before her hand limply shook the one Chastity held out. "Hello," she said quietly, although her eyes still held a glint of defiance.

"Now, if you'll excuse us, Cam, I'd like a drink please." Chastity tugged her hand free and smiled up at Cam.

"Of course." Cam smirked, almost pushing Brenda out of the way as they entered the ballroom.

"Wow." Stracey chuckled. "Hey, honey, you don't need me to ride shotgun. You've got this!"

Cam held her hand that was through his arm, giving it a slight squeeze. "Sorry," he apologized, his voice low and full of feeling.

"I assume that's one of the ones who's gonna have a broken heart tonight?" Chastity whispered.

"Afraid so." Cam nodded. "She's tried for a long time to get me to go out with her, and I may have slept around but I didn't do it on my own doorstep. I'm not *that* stupid."

Chastity snorted. "I hope not. However, if any of your conquests head my way, please give me a bit of warning."

"I will." Cam stopped a waiter, grabbing a couple of glasses of bubbly and passing them to the women before raising an eyebrow at Jinx.

"No." Jinx shook his head. "I want a real drink."

"Me too," Cam agreed, leading them towards the bar and ordering two whiskies.

"So . . ." Chastity looked around at the packed space, gowns of every shade and material before her, together with enough bling to blind a person. "What do we do? I'm still not quite sure."

"We buy tickets at an exorbitant price, then come and mingle, possibly bid on a silent auction or two, have far too many drinks, then there's music in another room for people that want to dance the night away. All rather boring really."

Chastity nodded. "I see. What are silent auctions and how do you participate?"

Cam looked over at the other side of the room. "There, see that table that's got people all

149

around it?" Chastity nodded. "That has a list of items that are up for auction and you write down which auction number and your bid and place it in the relevant box. At the end of the evening they announce who's won what and all monies raised go to the charity."

"Oh, can we go look?" Chastity sounded excited as Cam laughed.

"Sure." He started to lead her towards the auction table, only to be stopped time and again by people obviously wanting to know about the woman on his arm. Cam introduced her again and again as his fiancée and each time they were rewarded with shocked looks and gasps of surprise.

By the time they finally reached the table Chastity was finding it difficult to suppress her laughter. "I've really put the cat amongst the pigeons tonight, haven't I?"

"Yes," Cam chuckled. "Hopefully by tomorrow, word will have got around, gossip travels fast, and then everyone will know and we won't have to go through this again."

"I hope not." Chastity gave him a small smile. "I feel as if I'm on display for everyone. But I have to admit I'm enjoying all the funny looks from people when you introduce me."

"Me too." Cam admitted. "Now, you were wanting to see what was on offer, here, have a look through this."

Cam pointed to one of several leather bound books on the table. "If there's anything you fancy just give me the details and we can bid for it."

"Okay." Chastity placed her glass down and started flipping through the calligraphy covered pages that detailed everything that had been donated. She stopped at a couple for a moment, then flicked onwards quickly.

"Anything that grabs your attention?" Cam asked as he sipped his drink.

"Hmm, possibly, but I think I'd be able to get what I'm after in a normal store."

"What?" Cam asked, wondering what she could possibly need after their trip earlier.

"It's stuff for a baby . . ."

Cam gasped, grabbing her arm and turning her to him. "Are you?"

Chastity laughed. "No, sorry, didn't mean to scare you. It's for someone else but I don't want to say anything just yet as I'm pretty sure she's not told anyone."

"Who?" Cam raised an eyebrow.

"No, Cam." Chastity shook her head. "Honestly, I'm not saying anything at the moment. It's her choice when to tell people and the truth is she hasn't even told me. But I know. I always know when someone is pregnant, it's like a kinda gift."

"Okay, that's a bit weird." Cam cocked his head to the side. "Always? How? Is it scent?

Because I can usually do that too."

"No, it's not scent." Chastity shook her head then shrugged. "That comes later, when someone's a few weeks along, it's something else but I can't explain it."

"So you want to buy things for this baby you think may be coming?"

"Yes, I want to take them back when we return to the Packs."

Cam's shoulders rose and fell, his eyes twinkling. "Whatever you want. So, is there an auction that relates to babies?"

"Well, yes, but. . ."

"No buts, show me it and I'll bid. Remember it goes to the charity so I don't mind paying over the odds for whatever it is."

Chastity picked up the book, flipping back a few pages. "It's this one, it's for a 'newborn package' and includes clothes, a stroller that has interchanging bits so it's suitable from birth to toddler, and jeez, a whole host of other stuff. But it's from some fancy boutique and I'm sure I can get all this at a normal store at a fraction of the price."

"I'll bid on it. If my bid wins then all's good, if not, then you can get whatever you want from whichever store you want to shop in. Okay?"

Cam waited until she nodded then got the paper and pens provided and wrote the details of the auction down, together with an astronomical bid. He was pretty sure his would win, nobody in their right mind would bid more than what he'd written down. If they did then they were in dire need of some psychological aid. A small smile tugged at his lips as he placed the folded paper into the relevant box and turned back to his mate.

"All done." He couldn't help but grin as she smiled up at him. "I think we can safely say you'll win."

"What? Why?" Chastity frowned, tugging on his arm. "What did you do, Cam?"

"Moi? Nothing. Well, I did put in a rather large bid, so I think you'll win, honey."

"Cam! I could've got those things elsewhere, without spending a fortune."

"Yes, but this way the charity gets even more money from me. So, baby, it's a win win situation. Now, why don't we go and mingle a bit? There's several people I'd like you to meet."

Chastity nipped his arm, her nails digging in, as he moved them away from the throng around the auction table. "Oww, what was that for?"

"You could just have donated if you wanted the charity to get more money."

"Darling, I donate a ton of money to this particular charity." Cam leaned down, whispering in her ear. "I'm one of its patrons."

"Oh." Chastity shook her head. "You could just have told me that."

"Hey, it's hard keeping up with them all. I'm just breaking you in gently." Cam laughed as she pinched him again. "Stop it, we're supposed to be a newly engaged couple in love. Not an old married couple where the wife berates her husband."

"I wasn't berating you and," Chastity motioned with her finger, "come down here, I've decided."

Cam leaned down. "Decided what?"

Chastity kissed his ear before whispering softly. "I've decided where I want to get married. I want to do it in Rome, if that's okay with you?"

"Rome?" Cam's eyes widened. "That's a great idea and I assume you're doing it there so we don't have to go through the whole huge wedding thing here?"

"Partly," she admitted. "I want it to just be us two, nobody else."

"I don't think that's possible, honey." Cam shook his head. "I'm pretty sure no matter where we get married that we'll need witnesses. Plus, I don't think I want to get married without Jinx being there. He's been with me for a very long time and I want him there."

"Want me where?" Jinx butted in as he and Stracey joined them.

"Rome," Cam said. "Chastity wants us to tie the knot in Rome."

"Wonderful!" Jinx laughed. "I love Italy."

"Well, okay." Chastity kept her eyes on Cam. "Only Jinx and Stracey though, okay?"

"What?" Stracey asked as Cam kissed Chastity's head.

"Whatever you say, honey." He turned to Stracey. "Want to be one of the witnesses? Jinx, will you be my, whatever they call it, best man?"

Stracey giggled, clapping her hands with glee. "Rome! Italy! And a wedding to boot! What more could a girl ask for. Jinx, you better ready yourself for some shopping in those Italian boutiques. Leather, shoes, purses, oh the list is endless!"

Jinx groaned. "Damn, Sin, this is gonna cost me a fortune!"

Chastity laughed as Jinx tried to calm Stracey down. Cam clapped him on the shoulder. "No, it won't, it's for our wedding so the trip is on me, including the spending spree I suspect your mate is going to go on."

"Really?" Jinx asked, now smiling. "In that case, can I get one of those fancy Italian made-to-measure suits and some shoes? You know they make the best hand-made shoes there!"

Cam chuckled. "Whatever you want. Both of you, I mean it, I want this to be a trip we remember for a long time. Firstly, Stracey, you need to try and schedule it in and sort out any paperwork we'll need. You and Chastity can make any decisions on venue, hotel, whatever, just make sure we have enough time to spend a week or so there afterwards. I want us to have a proper honeymoon."

"Cam," Chastity bit her bottom lip nervously. "Hmm, if we're going all the way over there could we manage to visit Grant? I'd love to see Scotland, especially your home."

Jinx took Stracey by the elbow. "Time for us to go and be somewhere else. Anywhere else."

"Chastity, I know I agreed to us visiting but I was kinda thinking of a time in the future. Quite far in the future, honey." Cam sighed. "I don't want to see my father again so soon. It's complicated. He's complicated and our relationship is, well, I guess you'd say we're estranged but I'm hoping we can fix that in the future. I just don't want to see him yet, baby."

"I see." Chastity's eyes dropped. "Okay, if you feel like that then I understand, but, I'd feel real bad going all that way and not stopping to see Grant. So, I'll rethink on where we should get married. If that's okay?"

"We can still get married in Rome." Cam frowned. "I don't see what difference it makes."

"I know you don't." Chastity looked up at him through her thick lashes. "But it makes a difference to me. Can we agree we won't go to Rome until you're ready to visit Scotland?"

Sighing heavily Cam wrapped his arm

around her shoulders, his fingers soft on her skin. "I don't want to upset you, we can go to Rome later in the year. Once we're settled and got this Pack and business stuff running smoothly. By then I'm hoping I'll be able to return home without feeling I'm under his scrutiny. But, that still leaves us with the dilemma of where to hold our wedding."

"I'll think of something." Chastity leaned into his side.

"Okay, now, there are definitely people I need you to meet."

~ Chapter 13 ~

"I can't believe we won!" Chastity's voice full of excitement.

"I can." Cam laughed. "My bid was rather extravagant, even for that type of event."

"Well, I'm happy. Thank you."

Cam shrugged. "No problem. You wanted it so I made sure you got it."

Chastity smiled again, then frowned at Jinx. "What's wrong?" she asked, noticing his unhappy demeanor.

"So, no Rome?" Jinx moaned from his seat in the limo, now on their way home.

"Nope." Chastity shook her head. "But there is somewhere else I've always wanted to visit."

Cam pounced, at the ready to give her whatever she wanted. "Where? Tell me and I'll make it happen."

Chastity giggled. "It's not exactly Rome. In fact, it's as far removed from there as anything I can think of."

"Where?" Cam prodded again.

"Okay," Chastity took a deep breath. "No laughing allowed, but, it's Vegas. I've always wanted to go and I hear they do a lot of weddings there too."

The limo filled with Jinx and Stracey's laughter as Cam stared wide eyed at her. "Vegas? As in Las Vegas?"

Chastity nodded as Stracey gasped. "That's priceless! What better place for our Sin to get married than in Sin City!"

As Stracey's laughter took over again Chastity pouted. "You asked and I've told you. What's wrong with getting married in Vegas?"

Cam couldn't reply for a few moments, his mind envisioning a tacky, cheap, drive-through wedding chapel. When he finally managed to get words out he fought to control his own laughter. "Nothing, baby, if that's what you want then that's what we'll do."

"It is." Chastity confirmed, her jaw jutted out in defiance. "And I want to go to a show, a big show, with those dancers you see with feathers and huge headdresses."

"I can organize that." Stracey smiled, her laughter dying down, just a little. "We can organize it so it's done at a hotel, a nice hotel with a gazebo at the poolside, or in gardens. It doesn't need to be, sorry, Chastity, cheap 'n nasty. It can be a nice simple but elegant ceremony."

"What?" Cam frowned. "We can't do that! Chastity, honey, what do you say we get Elvis himself to marry us? After all, if we're doing it in Vegas then we should really do it Vegas Style! What do you think?"

Chastity clapped her hands, jumping up and

down on the leather seat. "Yes! Though I still just want Stracey and Jinx with us. Is that okay?"

Jinx still hadn't said a word because he was too busy laughing. Stracey's eyes were wide as she mouthed. "Elvis?"

Chastity reached over, patting Stracey's lap. "Yes! Elvis! It'll be fun and let's be honest, this isn't a wedding like a normal one. It's just for the human legal stuff. We're already married in every sense of the word so this is just getting it official for paperwork. Isn't it, Cam?"

"Well, yes, sort of." Cam sounded doubtful. "But I still wanted to give you a wedding you'd remember, honey."

"Cam!" Chastity grinned. "You think I'm gonna forget Elvis marrying us? It'll be something I'll remember, don't think it won't be."

"Okay, if that's what you want." Cam pulled her close. "But I insist on us staying somewhere really nice. I want you to experience the very best Vegas has to offer."

"I'll sort it. What's the timeframe, Cam?" Stracey asked, already going into assistant mode.

"We'll be here for another week then I have to go back and sort out some stuff at the Packs. I also want to get something up and running there that's in the works. So, what about a month at most six weeks from now, will that work for you, Chastity?"

"Sure." She smiled. "But, remember, before

we go back to the Pack, we've got that other business to take care of. For Jacob and Rebecca."

"Shit." Cam frowned. "I'd forgotten about that. We'll return to the Pack, so I can sort the outstanding situation with Fergie, and once I've done that we'll go and do that other thing."

"What?" Jinx had finally stopped laughing.

"It's nothing." Cam shook his head. "I promised Jacob we'd burn down that cabin we found Rebecca in. We're all going to do it, because Rebecca thinks the spirits of Bridget and that fucker might be lingering and she refuses to let Jacob and me go alone. And, this one here," Cam tugged Chastity close. "Well, she won't let me go without her. So the four of us will go and deal with it, once and for all."

"I see." Jinx's tone serious. "Maybe I should come?"

"No, it's okay." Cam shook his head. "I'd rather you and Stracey stayed in LA and carried on with work."

"You sure?" Jinx asked, obviously worried.

"I'm sure." Cam reiterated. "We're home. I'll see you two tomorrow. Stracey, we've got that conference call tomorrow and there's some other things I need to go over with you. I'll see you at ten, in my office."

"Okay, boss." Stracey let Jinx help her out of the limo as Cam helped Chastity out.

161

"Goodnight." Chastity waved as Stracey and Jinx started the short walk to her bungalow.

"See ya tomorrow." Jinx raised his hand as Stracey waved too.

"Now," Cam pulled her into his arms, kissing her for a brief moment. "Champagne, strawberries and a Jacuzzi are awaiting us. Hope you're not too tired?"

Chastity's eyes dilated, her voice soft. "Nope, I'm definitely not tired."

"Good." Cam laughed, picking her up and carrying her into the house.

His long legs strode across the entranceway, up the stairs and along the hall, turning to push the door open with his back, then entering their room. Cam walked to the center of the large room then placed her down on her feet, bending to kiss her deeply. Their lips locked, tongues invading each other's mouths, as his hand slid her gown's straps down. Cam forced his mouth from hers, breathing deeply he stared into her eyes.

"I adore you, my mate, with every fiber of my being."

Chastity reached up, her hand gently caressing his face. "Ditto, my mate. Now, are we going to eat those strawberries?"

Cam laughed, nodding. "Yes, but I've one more thing to do first."

Chastity pouted. "What?"

162

"This," he said, undressing her slowly and savoring every inch of her body as he did so. Once she stood naked before him he stepped back, his eyes intently looking at her soft skin. "Turn around."

His voice full of lust as Chastity turned, looking over her shoulder at him. "Every time I caught a glimpse of this." His finger traced her tattoo. "My heart leapt and, I hate to admit this, my cock twitched!"

"Really?" Chastity smirked. "I'll need to wear my hair up more often if that's the reaction I'm gonna get."

"Baby, I don't need to see your tattoo for my cock to harden." Cam bent to kiss her ink. "That happens just when I look at you. I have to admit though, the sight of you from behind turns me on, a lot! Your ass is just so fucking sexy."

"Well, my Alpha, this ass is getting cold. Can we get in the Jacuzzi?"

Cam laughed as he started to undress. "Give me a moment and I'll get the water running. Won't take but a few minutes to fill up and I'm pretty sure Kate's already left the champagne and strawberries in there. You can start on them while we wait."

"Good thinking, though I think only one more glass for me. I didn't realize, but, bubbly goes straight to my head. Very strange 'cause I can drink a ton of beer and it doesn't affect me in the least."

"I like you a little tipsy," Cam admitted,

already in the bathroom and turning the taps on, Chastity now sitting on the edge of the tub with a strawberry in her hand.

"Don't overfill it," she cautioned, a cheeky look in her eyes. "If you do then we'll make a mess of the floor."

"Will we now?" Cam teased, standing to remove the rest of his clothes.

"We will." She nodded, her eyes following his fingers as he slid his dress pants down over his thighs. "I see you wore underwear tonight. Hmm, I think I prefer it when you go commando."

"You're in a feisty mood tonight."

"Must be the champagne." She mused.

"If that's the case then I'm going to make sure you drink it more often."

Chastity giggled, sliding around to put her feet into the Jacuzzi. "That's divine." She moaned as Cam stood behind her, dropping to his knees and wrapping his arms around her.

"You're divine," he murmured against her throat, nipping and kissing along her shoulder.

"Can we go in yet?" she asked, quietly.

"Sure." Cam nodded as she slipped into the water.

"That's full enough." Cam grinned as he stepped in. "As you said, we don't want to make a mess."

He quickly turned the water off before laying

down in the middle of the large tub, pulling her to him she placed her legs either side of his thighs. "I see you're ready for me." She groaned as his fingers twirled around her already hard nipples.

"I'm always ready for you." Cam's hands moved to her waist, tugging her down so his manhood breached her entrance.

"Oh," Chastity gasped, settling around him before she moved upwards slowly.

Cam's head shot forward, his tongue fluttering over her breasts as she started to move in earnest. She braced her hands on his shoulders, using his body to help her movements. "Damn, that feels good," Cam groaned, his hands kneading her ass as she moved atop him.

"Fuck," Chastity cursed, her breathing shallow and quick as Cam moved an arm, his fingers now pressing against her clit. He kept the pressure up for a few moments before his fingers circled her nub, pressure and teasing combined to bring her to the brink.

Chastity increased her tempo, her eyes glassy as she almost purred. "More," she gasped as his fingers worked her clit.

Cam bit his lip, holding off his release to take her over into bliss. His ministrations causing her to yelp, gasp and scream, until finally she slammed herself down onto him and fell forwards. Her sheath contracted around him as he pushed his hips upwards, taking over for his mate, as she lay in his arms. As he thrust up into her she grabbed his hair, tugging to bring his lips to hers in a hot, passionate kiss. As her tongue darted inside his mouth his own release sped forwards, a long growl erupting from him to be lost in her mouth as his seed emptied inside her.

~ Chapter 14 ~

Logan laughed as Mason stood up, covered in dirt. "How many of those did you bring?"

"What? These?" Mason asked pointing to the plants he was placing all around the Camp. "Lots."

"Yes, I can see that." Logan looked around. "Where's Clayr? I've not seen much of her the last day or two."

"She's off with Ryder exploring. They're fast becoming good friends." Mason wiped his filthy hands on a rag he had tucked into his waistband.

"And that doesn't bother you? After all, we don't really know anything about him, although I plan on having a little talk with him later. I want some more details about him and his past. I feel, hmm, uneasy, yes, uneasy is the word I'd use. Not knowing a lot about the boy makes me wary."

"I can understand that." Mason shrugged. "But I've got a good feeling about him. He's good inside, if a little messed up. Clayr's told me a little about his life and it wasn't easy. He was shunned in the Pack for not being Wolf and he took it for as long as he could before he took off. He's been scavenging ever since just to survive."

"I'll probably agree with your assessment, Mason, but I need to see for myself. This Pack has gone through enough drama, we don't need any more."

167

Mason nodded. "I understand plus there's a few strange faces I noticed earlier. Who are they?"

Logan looked around the Camp, spotting one of the newcomers. "Mostly they're family of Pack members. Once word got out that Dupont was gone and the Pack was rebuilding, they came back. There's also one or two from other Packs that heard that Cam's looking to increase numbers and wanting strong, young, male Wolves. I've spoken to most of them and they appear to be okay. The last word will be Cam's though, but he's in LA for a week or so and won't be available to check them out until he returns. For now, I'm keeping an eye on things, and he's said if there's anything at all that seems 'off' I've got his permission to deny access to the Camp until he gets back. That's why I want to catch up with Ryder, I just want to get a sense of him and his intentions. He may be young but he's a Panther Shifter and I'm darn sure he's powerful."

"Yes," Mason agreed. "Clayr's told me he is fast and strong, but he's still a cub who's had a rough start. Try and take things easy with him, Logan. He's kinda shy too and he deserves a new home."

"I know." Logan bent his head to the side. "I'm not *that* scary and I'll go easy on him. I just haven't had the chance to talk to him properly yet."

Mason chuckled. "You're kinda intense, Logan. To a young cub that's had a bad start, aye, you are most definitely scary. Why don't you take

Tina with you when you talk to the boy? You always appear far more relaxed and happy when she's with you."

Logan's face lit up, a smile spreading across his face as Mason pointed a finger. "Aye, there it is. You completely change even at the mention of her name. So, how are things going with you two?"

"Slowly." Logan gave a lopsided grin. "We'll get there, it's just gonna take some time. She's a little upset 'cause Shelly's left with Grant, they shared a cabin so I'm moving in later. She says she feels safer when I'm near."

"I'm glad you're happy." Mason grinned. "I don't think I've ever seen you smile so much before. It's obvious to everyone how much you care for her."

"I do. I care so much it hurts. It hurts me that I wasn't around to protect her, you know, before."

Mason stepped closer, his hand gripping Logan's shoulder. "You can't do anything about the past, my friend. You can only shape the future and I know you'll make her happy. I'm sure I even saw her smile a few times yesterday."

"Yes," Logan agreed. "She's learning that she can relax, that's she's safe, and that I won't let anything happen to her. I'd die protecting her and the Goddess herself couldn't save anyone that hurt her again."

Mason stepped back. "Wow, that was rather heartfelt. I could feel your anger rising there,

Logan."

"Sorry." Logan's shoulders lifted and dropped quickly. "I can't help it. Just the thought of someone doing harm to her makes my blood boil."

"I can see that." Mason turned back to what he'd been doing, sinking down to his knees in the dirt. "I better get back to this. I want everything done for when Cam comes again. I think he'll like it."

"I'm sure he will," Logan agreed. "If you can let Ryder know I'm looking for him, I'd appreciate it."

"Will do." Mason didn't look up, intent on the job at hand.

"See you later," Logan said as he walked away, doing his rounds of the Camp and making sure all was as it should be. "Oh, wait, I meant to ask, can you meet me later to go over some security for the Camp? I want to get shifts set up so that there's always at least two or three Wolves on duty."

"Sure can. Just come and find me, or, better still, why don't you and Tina join us for dinner? Clayr will be there and probably Ryder. Monique's been making food for us and bringing it over. She's even stayed to eat with us a few times."

"Sounds good. We'll see you then." Logan waved as he turned away thinking, *Two birds with one stone.*

He carried on with his duties, ensuring Pack safety, including checking up on the guards that were posted. Two of the Wolves were new to the job so he tried his best to sneak up on them and although he got very close, they both were snarling and growling in response to his surprise visit. Logan nodded at them both and went on his way to make sure everything and everyone was safe.

He knew he was serious and, as Mason had put it, intense, but meeting Tina had brought out a softer side to him that he hadn't even known was there. Logan pondered on their situation, knowing his mate-to-be was in a fragile state and that he had to take things slowly or he'd scare her away. Although Tina admitted she was aware that he was her soul-mate, she was still scared to take the next step between them. Her fear of what had happened to her holding her back.

She'd explained that what she was scared of was that what she'd gone through would somehow affect the way she was with him, in an intimate way, and she couldn't bear to hurt him; just as much as he couldn't bear to hurt her. Catch twenty two situation. Logan prayed to the Goddess each night to help her get over her fears so they could start their new life together, properly, so he could show her just how much he cared for her. *"It'll happen when she's ready,"* he told himself as he now went in search of her. Thinking about Tina as he'd made his rounds brought a deep need to see her, touch her, hold her in his arms and make certain she was okay.

Logan broke into a gentle jog, then picked up speed to a slow run, again his speed increased, his feet running flat out over the forest floor as he sought her out. As he broke free of the trees he saw her making her way towards him, a gentle smile on her face. Tina's pace increased as they drew closer, Logan slowing so he wouldn't knock her off her feet as his arms clamped around her and held her tight.

"You okay?" she asked, her voice muffled against his chest.

"Aye," Logan sighed. "I'm okay now. I missed you, my bonnie lass."

"I missed you too." Tina pulled away slightly to look up at him. "I could sense you, Logan, that's why I came looking for you. Are you sure everything's okay?"

"Yes," Logan reaffirmed. "I was worried you'd still be upset about Shelly leaving."

"I am," she confirmed. "But, I have you now and I wondered if we could go and get your stuff to move it into mine?"

"Yes." Logan laughed. "I think that's a grand idea."

"Good." Tina pulled out of his arms, grabbing a hand and tugging him along. "I hope you like staying in my place, it's smaller than most of the cabins, but it was big enough for Shelly and me."

"It'll be just fine, Tina." Logan smiled, seeing the twinkle in her eyes, one that had been slow to arrive and take away the hollow, sad, look that had haunted her. "Plus, we don't have to cook tonight, we're having dinner with Mason."

"We?" Tina frowned, looking a little confused.

"Yes, we. We are having dinner at Mason's."

Tina shook her head. "That's not what I meant. You said 'we don't have to cook'?"

Logan chuckled. "Aye, I'm quite adept in the kitchen. In fact, I love cooking, so you won't be doing all of it. We can cook together and I'll even cook your meals for you. I'm particularly good at scrambled eggs and crispy bacon for breakfast."

Tina stopped, her eyes blinking rapidly in surprise. "Really?"

"Yes, really." Logan pulled her onward. "I know a lot of Wolves stay out of the kitchen, but, I've always liked cooking so mother taught me. She said, and I quote, *'It's aboot time the men in this Pack learned their way aboot a kitchen.'* She was giving dad the evil eye when she said it."

"Well, hotdamn!" Tina laughed. "I don't think I've ever seen a male of this Pack cooking. Well, unless it's one of our celebrations and it's roasting meat on the open fire pit, or barbecue, but certainly not in a kitchen."

"I know most don't, but I do." Logan shrugged. "A couple of the other guys used to tease me back home but they soon stopped."

Tina's head tilted to the side as she raised an eyebrow. "Why did they 'soon stop'?"

"I woulda thought that was obvious." Logan looked deadly serious. "'Cause I kicked their proverbial backsides from one end of the Camp to the other. Then I stopped, turned to everyone watching, and asked if there was anyone else who thought I was a sissy for learning to cook." Logan's lips twitched up, his eyes sparkling. "Nobody answered and from then on they never commented on it again."

Tina giggled, a proper giggle, the first in a very long time. Her eyes filled with tears as her arms held her sides as Logan just stared for a moment or two before joining her. Several moments later she managed to take a deep breath and speak. "Boy, I wish I'd been there. You're an amazing man, my Highland lad."

"Aye, well, I knew if I didn't stop it straight away it'd be like a freight train and soon I'da been fighting every day. One good fight where I kicked their behinds . . ."

"Their?" Tina queried. "There was more than one?"

"Hell, aye, there were three to begin with. Two brothers who were always looking for trouble, trying to bully the younger cubs, and one of their friends." Logan looked off into the distance, as if remembering the moment in time. "I was on my own to start, but, with the noise and such there was soon a crowd. Rory appeared, running like a madman and howling like some crazy guy. He just bowled right into their friend and that left me with the brothers."

Logan stopped, a small smile creeping onto his face. "Well, they were no different than any other bully I've ever come across. All talk and only able to hurt others when they have the numbers and size on their side. They were a bit older than me but I've always been big for my age and our dad taught us well when it came to fighting. So, I took the two of them on and won. I won't say I wasn't hurt because I was. A cornered bully is about as dangerous as a rabid dog, double that, and well, it was a long, dirty fight. Mum gave me a clout round the ears when I finally got home because she used our steaks that were for dinner and put them on my mashed up face. Then she hugged me tight and told me how proud she was that I'd stood up to them. Was kinda weird afterwards 'cause they stayed well clear of me and they stopped bullying as much. I guess they realized I wouldn't let them get away with it any longer."

Tina's hand reached up, her fingers trailing down the side of his face. "You're a good man, Logan. I guess that started young in you, I mean, the need to help others. I think it's in your DNA and I hope to meet your mum and dad someday. Will you take me? To visit your Highland home and meet your parents?"

Logan's hand came up to cover hers, moving so he kissed her palm. "Damn right I will. I'd be so proud to show you off back in Scotland. All the others will be jealous of the beauty I've snared."

Tina's face blushed, starting on her neck and moving up quickly to cover her face. "Shush, it's me that's got the best deal here. Now, shall we go and get your stuff. I can't wait to see your things in our home. It's goin' to make it more, oh I don't know, permanent isn't the word I'm looking for, but I think you understand what I mean. Don't you?"

Logan smiled down into her upturned face, leaning to place a gentle kiss at the side of her mouth. "Yes, I do." He nodded and pulled back. "Let's go and do this. Oh, you know I sleep on the side closest to the door. Is that okay?"

A shadow fell over her face and she nodded quickly. "Yes, that's more than okay. I tend to sleep as far away from the door as I can."

As they started to walk Logan thought on her words, the sadness and fear that had flitted across her face. "From now on, Tina, I'm going to be between you and the door. You don't need to feel scared anymore."

"I know that." Tina nodded. "I do, it's just hard to really believe they're all gone. I keep expecting to wake up and find it's all a dream."

Logan pulled on her hand, spinning her around in front of him before picking her up and cradling her in his arms. "No dream. I'm here, I'm real, and I'm bloody well staying."

"Logan! Put me down. What will folks think?"

Logan shook his head. "I don't give a flying fuck what anyone thinks. I'm carrying my mate and that's all there is to it. Now, cuddle in 'cause I'm not putting you down again until we're home. When we get there, you will go and have a nice long bath, get ready for our first 'dinner date' and I'll go and get my stuff from the Club House. Okay?"

"More than okay, Logan." Tina's arms snaked around his neck as he carried her the rest of the way to their cabin.

Leaving her to go and have a bath, Logan returned to the room he'd been using and quickly packed up his things before walking the short distance back. His critical eye seeing a few repairs that needed doing on the cabin as he drew closer. He was also going to ask Mason to work his magic with the outside, planting some flowers to make the place more colorful and homey. Logan saw several ways to make the place nicer, better, more fitting to house his mate, and he'd get to work the very next day. He also hoped that Mason still had some of his 'surprises' left so they could be dotted around the outside. It would set the place off and make it look wonderful.

Pushing the door open with his foot he

entered the cabin, stopping just inside to savor the moment. A moment that he knew he'd remember for a long time, if not forever; this second when he and his mate started their life living together. A long sigh escaped him as a smile stretched his lips wide, his eyes savoring every detail before he moved an inch. Tina's singing brought him out of his reverie, kicking off his dirty boots, he moved forwards, toward the sound.

Her voice sounded happy, carefree, as he placed his things on the floor of the bedroom before heading towards the attached bathroom. Peeking inside he saw Tina, lying back in a mass of bubbles, her eyes closed and singing. Logan didn't know the song, it sounded like a lullaby that a mother would sing to her child, but it didn't matter. What did matter was the relaxed way Tina lay, her face soft, radiant, with no hint of fear in her beautiful features.

"Hey," Logan spoke quietly, not wishing to scare her.

Tina sat up, laughing. "Damn, you caught me singing."

"Yes, I did." Logan stayed at the door, desperate to enter, but firmly keeping his feet still. "What were you singing?"

"My mom used to sing it to me when I was little and for some reason it just came to me." She turned, looking over her shoulder.

Logan's breath caught in his chest at her

beauty, her skin looked so soft, but he still didn't enter. By sheer force of will, he didn't rush to her to pick her up and crush her naked body to his. In fact, this was his first glimpse of her naked and he fought to control his reaction to the sight. Unfortunately, his manhood totally ignored him and within seconds he was hard and uncomfortable.

"If you want to come in, you can." Tina spoke shyly, her eyes lowering as her face flushed.

"I don't need to." Logan hoped she couldn't see his cock straining to break free. "If you're not comfortable with me coming in, I can go and unpack."

"I think I'd like you to." Tina's eyes flitted up to his, her smile nervous. "In fact, could you come wash my back?"

Logan didn't wait for her to change her mind, rushing over and dropping to his knees beside the bath. "Sure. Here, give me the sponge and soap."

Tina handed them over before pulling her knees up and leaning forward to clasp her arms around them. "Thank you," she murmured as Logan started to soak her back.

"My pleasure." Logan managed to get out, his arousal growing by the second.

"Logan, I want to say thank you, for being so patient with me." Tina's head moved to the side, resting on her arms as she stared at him. "I know it's not been easy for you."

179

"Hey, you don't need to thank me for doing the right thing, and the right thing is for me to look after my mate. If that means we're taking things slow then that's okay, Tina. Please, bonnie lass, don't ever think I'll push you into doing something you're not ready for."

"I know that." Tina smiled. "I can feel you sometimes, your love, your caring. You're pretty amazing, Logan. Not many men would be as tolerant as you've been and I know that."

Logan stopped washing her soft skin, moving to stroke her cheek. "I'll wait forever for you."

"I don't think that'll be necessary." Tina laughed. "I think I'm ready but I'm just a little scared."

"We don't need to take things further right now. Not if you're scared, honey."

"I'm not scared of you, Logan." Tina shook her head. "I'm scared I can't be the woman you deserve. I'm . . ."

Logan leaned over, kissing her gently before pulling back. "Don't give them that. Don't allow them to sour your life, Tina. You're gorgeous, strong, kind and brave, you are everything any Wolf could ask for in a mate and I know how lucky I am to have found you. If you're not ready then we'll wait. Simple solution."

Tina stared hard into his face, her eyes taking

in every detail before her fingers traced his lips. "I'm ready," she whispered, pulling him towards her and kissing him deeply.

Logan's heart soared, his beast roared, as he felt her passion grow. His senses on high alert for any nervousness, any fear, but he found none. Her arousal was rising to meet his and he reluctantly pulled away. The soft moan that fell from her lips causing him to grin. "I think we need to move to the bedroom or we're gonna make a hell of a mess in here."

He grabbed a towel and held it out as Tina rose from the water, stepping out of the bath and into his arms. Logan folded the towel around her before picking her up and carrying her back into their room. "Here, let me dry you." He almost groaned as his hands slid over her body, gently rubbing the towel all over her skin.

Logan took great care to be gentle, not rushing his movements as he continued to dry every inch of Tina's body. Her little groans and moans made his heart leap in his chest as he realized they were going to finally seal their bond. He was aware that he would mark her, he knew he wouldn't be able to stop himself and a moment's panic roared through him.

"What's wrong?" she asked, sensing his unease.

"I don't think I'll be able to stop myself from

marking you, from sealing our bond, Tina." Logan's hands stilled, holding her in place as he stared into her liquid pools. "I don't want to scare you but I don't think I'll be able to not fulfill our mating."

"I know." Tina nodded. "I'm well aware of how you feel, Logan, I feel the same. Please, believe me when I tell you that you don't scare me. I feel the safest I've felt in a long time when I'm with you."

"What if my bite hurts?" he asked, knowing he desperately wanted to sink his fangs into her soft skin.

"What if mine hurts you?" she asked shyly.

"Yours?" he asked, surprised. "You want to mark me too?"

"Hell yeah," Tina smirked. "I'm kinda excited about it. I want to bite you so bad it hurts."

"Well, that's a relief." Logan grinned. "Why don't you get into bed while I get undressed?"

"No." Tina shook her head. "I think I want to do that. After all, it's the first time I'll be seeing all of you. Sleeping in the same bed while still clothed doesn't count. So, Logan, please let me."

Logan didn't answer as her hands started to lift his t-shirt, her fingers trailing across his skin, he couldn't speak, holding his breath in anticipation. He raised his arms and helped her to remove it, her hands letting it fall to the floor as her eyes raked across his chest.

"What's this? Is this your Clan tattoo I've

heard about?" Her eyes locked on the ink over his heart.

"Yes." The word coming out in a strangled groan.

"And what are these?" Her fingers caressed his skin as it traced his tribal tattoo before lowering to his twin tattoos.

"The first is just one I liked but those two are ones representing Rory and me. I'm the blue and Rory is the yellow. It was a way for folks to tell us apart when we were younger."

"I like them, all of them." Tina pressed a small kiss to his Clan tattoo before dropping to kiss the yellow of his twin tattoo.

"Damn." Logan's body tensed as her lips flitted over his skin. "Tina, I think we should get into bed."

"In a minute." Tina stood, staring up at him as her hands undid his jeans. "I need to undress you, remember?"

"You better hurry up, lass, or I'm goin' to burst."

Tina unfastened the button, lowered the zipper, and pushed his jeans down. Her eyes went wide as his manhood popped free, now unrestrained and throbbing with need. "Commando?" she chuckled.

"Yeah." Logan stepped out of his jeans, dropped the towel he still held in one hand, and pulled her towards him. "Bed." He led her over to the large bed and as she crawled onto it he moaned aloud, biting his bottom lip at the sight of her naked ass.

"I'll try and take things slow, but, I'm not goin' to lie, Tina, it's goin' to be hard."

"It's already hard." Tina nodded toward his cock as he got in beside her.

"Hell, it's been hard so many times over the past few weeks that I thought I'd do myself an injury."

Tina laughed. "Is that even possible?"

"No feckin' idea but it sure felt as if I was." Logan pushed Tina onto her back, raising himself over her as his mouth sought hers. As their bodies merged, lips joining, tongues dancing, and hearts beating wildly, Logan thought he'd died and gone to heaven. He restrained himself, teasing her with his mouth and hands, caressing her breast, and settling on her nipple, slowly twirling it between his fingers.

"Oh!" she gasped into his mouth. "Logan, please!"

"What?" he murmured against her lips.

"I need you to claim me." She almost cried as she thrust her hips towards him.

Logan pulled back, his eyes locked on hers. "Are you certain, my bonnie lass?"

"Yes!" she squealed as he pushed her thighs apart, slowly entering her warmth.

Logan couldn't help the low growl that escaped, rumbling up his chest and out of his throat without thought. "You're so warm, welcoming, and you fit me just right. You're perfect, Tina, absofreakinglutely perfect."

Tina's eyes stared into his, her pupils dilated to darken them even further than her normal chocolate pools. A soft smile lifted her lips as she joined his movements, meeting his thrusts flawlessly, as her own arousal grew. He knew, because he could scent it clearly as their passion grew. Their breathing increased, sweat soaking their bodies as they soared higher and higher, Logan's fangs erupted from his gums as a roar fell from his lips.

Still he held himself in check, his self-restraint astounding him as he fought to breathe deeply. "Are you sure?" he barely got out, not wanting to scare her, or hurt her, so deeply ingrained in him that he succeeded in holding himself in check.

"Yes!" she gasped, her own razor sharp canines making a quick appearance. Tina grabbed the hair at the back of his head, tugging him to place his mouth over her soft skin.

Logan's breath flew from him as Tina bit down hard on his skin, tearing through and clamping onto him fiercely. His beast reacted to the bite, his mouth fastening onto her silky skin, a second before his fangs punctured it and sank deep inside. As her sweet blood touched his tongue he growled deeply with ecstasy, and then he felt it, deep down inside him, right in his core; their bond cementing.

Logan's head reared back, an immense roar tearing from his throat as their release overtook them both. Tina screaming his name brought such a sense of completion to him that he roared again with happiness. When her sheath stopped contracting around him, he slowly pulled out, falling to her side and grasping her tight in his arms.

"I love you, my mate." Logan's voice soft, caring, and sincere. "I won't let anything or anyone hurt you again. I promise."

"Logan," Tina stuttered. "I can't believe how that made me feel. Did you feel it? When we marked each other, did you feel it?"

"Yes, my bonnie lass, I felt it." Logan's tone full of love as he kissed the top of her head. "Our bond is almost complete. All we need now is our ceremony and we'll be bound together for eternity."

"I can't even put into words how I feel about you, Logan." Tina's eyes filled with tears as she fought to control her emotions. "It's more than love, it's more than anything I've ever felt before. Love doesn't seem enough to describe it."

"I know." Logan's finger wiped a stray tear from her cheek. "It's a little overwhelming, isn't it?"

"Uh uh," Tina gulped. "I'm sorry I took so long to take this step."

"No," Logan shook his head. "Don't ever think that, darlin'. I'da waited far longer for you, however long it took, I woulda still been here waiting."

"I know that, Logan." Tina smiled. "That's what makes you so special."

"You're the special one." Logan kissed her nose quickly, grinning like the proverbial Cheshire Cat.

Tina looked shyly up at him. "Do we really need to go to Mason's for dinner?"

Logan nodded. "Afraid so. I really need to catch up with Ryder and check him out. He always seems to avoid me and I won't relax until I've sussed him out."

"Oh, I see." Tina's eyes popped wide. "I meant to tell you, my cousin Nate is coming home. He and his mate, Brett, left soon after Dupont and his men arrived 'cause they treated them real bad. Said they weren't Pack, not real Wolves, 'cause they were together. Said proper Wolves mated to bring more cubs to a Pack and that they were less than useless. It got physical a few times and after Brett got beat by Dupont and some of his men, they decided to leave. It broke my heart as Nate is the kindest, most loveable person that you could ever meet."

Logan scowled. "What? What kind of nonsense is that? Love is love, a mate is a mate, no matter who or what they are. I can't believe how some Packs still ostracize same sex matings. We've never done that, not in the history of Highland Wolf Clan. We accept everyone, no matter their creed, color, or choice in mates."

"I know," Tina agreed. "Nate and Brett are so much in love, it's a joy just to see them together and they always worked hard within the Pack. They are fabulous hunters and kept the Pack's meat stocks topped up. We never had to worry when they were here, they were always out getting something or other for us."

"Well, I'll welcome them with open arms 'cause we can always do with keeping the stores topped up."

"Thank you." Tina's fingers ran over his naked abs, trailing around his tattoos. "I appreciate that. I told him they would be welcome and he sounded excited to come home. They've been gone for so long and I told him about you, he said he needed to check you out." Tina laughed. "He's adorable, but he's all the family I have left so it'll be nice to have him back again."

"I would expect nothing less of your next of kin, baby. He has a right to make sure I'll treat you properly and back home, in Scotland, it's common practice for a close family member to give a mate a good 'seeing to' as we put it. Which generally means we make sure they know the consequences of mistreatment of our females."

"Really?" Tina laughed. "I can see you doing that. Doing the whole protective thing."

"Yeah." Logan shrugged. "Hey, Rory and I have put the fear of the Goddess into quite a few Wolves in the past. One of us is bad enough but the two of us together can be quite . . . overpowering."

"I can imagine," Tina agreed. "I know Rory comes across as fun-loving, but he's also dangerous and strong. Like you."

"I hope I don't make you feel I'm dangerous?"

"No!" Tina shook her head. "That's definitely not how you are with me, but, at the same time I know it's there and I know it would come out if needed. Which is good, Logan, it makes me feel safe."

"I'm glad." Logan's fingers trailed down her side, causing her to shiver. "I always want you to feel safe."

"Logan . . ." Tina's eyes locked with his. "How long do we have before we need to go to Mason's?"

Logan grinned then chuckled. "Oh, not for a few hours yet."

"Well, that's good, 'cause I'd like a repeat performance, my mate."

"No." Logan shook his head as he turned Tina onto her back, his hands moving over her body.

189

"I'm taking things much slower this time. I want to worship every last," he kissed her shoulder before moving downwards, his lips caressing her breast. "inch of you." Logan sucked her nipple into his mouth, Tina's back arching as she moaned. "Every," he moved further down, kissing her belly, "single inch."

As Logan felt her body respond to him he smiled against her skin. "I'm going to let you know how much I adore you."

His lips hovered over her apex, blowing slightly straight onto her most sensitive area. The strangled groan of pleasure it elicited causing him to smile. "Just lie there and let me show you, my bonnie lass, show you exactly how it should be between us."

"Yes." Tina whimpered as Logan's tongue darted out to tease her mercilessly.

~ Chapter 15 ~

"Don't." Logan held out a hand, stopping Tina from putting a scarf around her neck.

"Logan, I'm covered in your bites. Everyone will know what we've been up to."

"I know." Logan pulled her into his arms. "That's the point."

Tina laughed, a soft tinkling sound that was music to his ears. "Logan, you are incorrigible."

"Sorry." Logan shrugged. "What's your point? I want everyone to know you're my mate, and I am yours, hence this t-shirt."

Logan fingered the black t-shirt that hung low around his neck, clearly showing her bites on his skin. "I've waited for ages for this, my mate. Please don't cover your marks up."

"Okay." Tina dropped the scarf. "But I'm telling you now, if my face is in a constant state of blushing then you will need to make it up to me when we get home."

"It will be my pleasure!" Logan laughed, pulling her along behind him. "We better go or Mason will come looking for us."

"I assume Clayr will be there?" Tina asked, skipping to keep up with Logan's long strides. "I like her, she's nice, even if she's quite a bit younger than me. I think we'll become good friends."

"Yes," Logan answered. "She'll be there, and

191

hopefully Ryder too. Monique's been cooking for them and bringing dinner over each evening. I spoke to her yesterday and she says Ryder is settling in well. He's helping her with chores but he spends a lot of time out with Clayr. Those two are fast becoming best friends and I just want to make sure he's no threat, to Clayr, or the Pack."

"He's just a kid." Tina countered.

"A Panther Shifter is what he is, Tina." Logan stopped on the porch, turning to look intently at her. "He may be young, but he could still be a threat. I just want to make sure we've not made a mistake in taking him in."

"I know you take the security of the Pack seriously, but really? He's had a hard start to life so he's going to be guarded, but I don't think he's any kind of threat. I feel sorry for him."

Logan pulled her closer, cuddling her quickly before releasing her and continuing, "I know you do, that's what makes you such a wonderful person. But it's my job to make sure everyone is safe and I won't shirk that duty."

"I understand." Tina squeezed his hand. "I know you take it seriously, Logan. All I'm saying is don't go too hard on Ryder, that's all, remember he's little more than a cub and he's bound to be wary of us after the start in life he's had."

"I'll try." Logan shrugged. "I guess I can be a little intense at times."

"Well, I'm here to help you. If you don't mind that is?"

Logan stopped again, turning to gaze down at Tina. "Of course I don't mind. I can't promise to always take your advice, but I'll try. That doesn't mean you stop giving me it, just that sometimes we may not agree, and that's okay, Tina. We don't have to have the same opinion all the time. Just because we may not see eye to eye sometimes doesn't mean I won't appreciate your help."

"Okay." Tina gave a shy smile. "It's kinda weird getting used to all this, isn't it?"

"Yes," Logan agreed. "But we'll learn together and I think we're going to make a damn fine team. Now, come on, I'm starving and I need lots of food. Lots. 'Cause I'm sure I'm going to need it for energy. After all, this will be our first official night as bonded mates and I plan on taking you to heights you never imagined."

"Logan!" Tina exclaimed, looking all around as her face blushed. "Shush! We're in the middle of a Camp of Wolves, ya know? Super sensitive hearing and all that!"

"What?" Logan teased. "I'm not allowed to shout from the rooftops what I plan on doing to you later?"

"No!" Tina's hand shot up, covering his lips. "Shhh, not another word. I mean it!"

"Okay, let's go eat then." Logan walked on.

"If I'm eating then my mouth is busy doing something other than talking."

"Good idea." Tina giggled as they walked up to the door of the Pack House where Mason and Clayr were staying.

Logan pushed the door open, shouting as he entered. "Mason, you here?"

"Aye," Mason replied. "We're in the kitchen. I was just about to come find you, dinner's ready."

Tina held back, her face showing her embarrassment as Logan pulled her after him. "I'm starving." Logan said as they entered the kitchen to find Mason, Clayr, Ryder and Oliver, another new Highlander, seated and tucking into a pile of food.

Clayr turned to say a quick "Hello." When her eyes fell to Tina's neck. She jumped up, squealing and rushing over to hug Tina tightly. "Oh my gosh! You two have finally got 'round to marking each other! Congratulations."

Tina was dumbstruck, her face scarlet as Clayr looked at Logan, grinning and pointing to his neck. "I see you're wearing them with pride, Logan."

Mason and Oliver joined them, shaking hands, clapping backs and staying well clear of Tina. "Aye, I am that," Logan replied, his smile wide as he pulled Tina close to his side. "Stay away, boys, 'cause I'm at the ripping out throats stage."

Oliver went back to his seat, laughing as Mason held his hands up. "No worries, my friend.

194

I'm happy for you both, but what the hell are you doing here? You should be locked up tight in your cabin."

Logan shrugged. "I wanted to let you all know, plus I'm starving."

Mason ushered them forward. "I think you two should sit at the other end of the table, but there's plenty of food so tuck right in."

Logan took Tina to the farthest away seats, sitting down and shuffling his seat closer to hers. "Pass us some plates, Ryder." Logan's eyes watched the youngster as he moved quickly to do his bidding.

"Thanks," Logan said as he took them from the young Panther.

"Here." Mason pushed bowls of food towards them. "Looks like you're gonna need this."

Tina blushed again, pinching Logan in the side as he laughed. "Thank you, now, how is everyone? Oliver, you settling in alright?"

"Sure." Oliver's head bobbed up and down, his red hair falling over his eyes. "It's not that much different to home. Well, except for all the wildlife that is. Bears! There's feckin' bears in the forest, Logan."

"I know." Logan chuckled. "And lots more that we don't have. It's great hunting here."

"What?" Ryder looked between them. "You don't have bears?"

"No." Logan shook his head. "We've not had

bears in the wild for a very long time. But, you know all about how dangerous they are, don't you?"

"Hell, yeah." Ryder nodded quickly. "They can be scary up close. I usually stay away from them, well, I try to."

"Good advice." Logan looked back to Oliver. "Take the lad's advice, unless hunting as a Pack, stay well clear."

"Don't need to tell me twice." Oliver sipped his beer. "I saw one yesterday and hightailed it away quick as I could go. It was a female with a cub, doubly dangerous. But it was exciting to actually see one in the flesh. They're beautiful, scary, but beautiful."

"Yes," Logan agreed before turning to Ryder. "So, how are you? Is Monique treating you okay?"

Ryder looked down at his plate, mumbling, "Yes, she's really nice, but she treats me like a cub. She's given me a curfew. Can you believe that? I'm not a baby."

Logan smirked, looked to Mason who was also grinning, before replying, "A curfew is good, Ryder. You're definitely not a baby, but, you aren't much more than a cub in her eyes. She's only trying to look after you."

"I know that," Ryder muttered. "It's just strange. I've never had anyone care enough to impose something like a curfew on me."

"Never?" Logan asked before he could stop

himself.

Ryder's eyes met his and Logan saw the pain and hurt in the young Shifter's. "No, never. I was kinda left to my own devices for as long as I can remember. So, no, Logan, I've never lived in a Pack like this, never had anyone look out for me, and I gotta admit it feels weird. I'm sorry, but what is it you want from me? There must be something. Nobody does anything for nothing, so I'm just waiting to find out what all this is gonna cost me."

Logan's eyes flew to Mason's, then Clayr's, then back to Ryder's. He took a moment to respond to the shocking revelation that this boy was expecting to pay for his keep in some way. "Ryder," Logan sighed then felt Tina's hand on his thigh, gently squeezing it. "We don't want anything from you, apart from loyalty to the Pack. We all work together to make the Pack strong and to protect it from any harm. We look after everyone, whether they are young or old, and we sure as hell aren't looking for payment from you. For anything. All I want to know is if you're happy, healthy and willing to help the Pack. That's it. No hidden agenda."

Clayr punched Ryder's arm. "Told ya," she said as Ryder still stared at Logan.

"Sorry, if I've offended you, but," Ryder sighed, his youth showing through his bravado. "I'm still a little suspicious. My dealings with Packs in the past haven't been anything like this and I keep waiting on the punchline."

Logan sat up straighter, his tone a little harsher. "I'll say this only once more, Ryder, but before I do I'll let you into a secret . . . I don't lie." Logan paused, raising an eyebrow at the youngster. "So, again, we do not want anything from you in payment for housing, food, clothes or anything else you need. You'll be looked after as any other Wolf who is a member of the Pack. We look after our own, and we do not take advantage of anyone. Is that perfectly clear, Ryder?"

Clayr prodded Ryder. "Uh oh, you've made him mad. I told you, Highlander's take their word very seriously. It's a personal insult if you think they're lying. Say you're sorry, Ryder. Please."

Mason looked between Logan and the Panther, obviously waiting to see how his sister's friend would react. Logan kept his gaze on Ryder, his jaw clenched at the insulting way the boy had questioned his intentions. Ryder's eyes blazed with defiance for a moment before his stare lowered.

"Sorry," Ryder mumbled as Clayr let out a pent up breath.

"Logan. . ." Clayr started but stopped when Mason placed a hand on her arm.

"Ryder," Logan's tone a little softer. "I understand you've not lived within a good, decent Pack. But, and I stress this again, we pride ourselves on how we act as a Pack. From the Alpha down, we have a code of conduct that dictates how we behave. It's fairly simple—look after the Pack and the Pack will look after you. We do not act with disregard to our fellow Wolves, we look after those too weak to look after themselves, and we do not, under any circumstances, take advantage of anyone."

Clayr prodded Ryder in the side, the young Panther throwing her a scowl before he turned back to Logan. "I apologize. I'm not used to all . . . this." His hand waved in front of him. "It's hard to get used to."

Logan relaxed, his senses telling him Ryder wasn't trying to hide anything, what he felt from him was . . . shock, unease, and a little fear. "I understand. If you ever have anything you need to talk to me about then come and find me. I'll do my best to help you integrate into the Pack. My main duties are making sure we're all safe and everything is running as it should be. So, Ryder, welcome to the Pack. I hope you'll be happy here."

Ryder's lips twitched up a little, a faint smile on his face as he nodded. "Thank you. I'll try and help if I can. I'm fast and a good tracker, I've had to be."

Clayr piped up enthusiastically. "He freakin' is! I can barely keep up with him and you guys know how fast I am."

"That we do." Mason sneered. "It's how you keep giving me the slip!"

Oliver laughed, almost choking on his beer. "Damn, it's true though. Clayr is one fast cub."

Clayr glowered over the table before throwing a piece of bread at Oliver. "Hey! Technically, I've not been a cub for a few years! I'm an adult now, ya eejit!"

"Ooops," Oliver grinned. "Sorry, little one. I keep forgetting."

"Well don't!" Clayr was still angry, glaring over the table. "I'm old enough to be mated if I want to be!"

Mason growled, low, but everyone heard it. "Don't talk like that, Clayr. You are *not* getting mated."

Clayr turned to her brother, raising her hands up and then dropping them to hit the table. "I didn't say I wanted to! Only that I'm old enough. You lot need to stop treating me like a baby."

Ryder sniggered. "Now you know how I feel."

Spinning around quickly Clayr pushed him hard. "Hey! One, you're supposed to be on *my* side, and, two, you're younger than me!"

"Maybe," Ryder smirked. "But I've been on my own for more than two years, fending for myself without a Pack. Looks like you've got a horde of Wolves looking after you."

Mason nodded. "Indeed she has, Panther, so just you remember that."

"What?" Ryder's eyes widened in shock. "No, no and no! Clayr's my friend, that's it."

Clayr punched him hard this time, her face red as a beetroot. "Oh for goodness sake! Again, one, I'm waaaaaaaaaaay out of your league, and, two, you're too young for me! I'll be looking for a man, not a boy."

Mason growled again, his face surly as he stared hard at Clayr. "Will you just stop? Now, please, before I have a heart attack, or worse."

Clayr laughed. "Worse? What would be worse?"

"Me ripping someone's throat out." Mason raised an eyebrow as Oliver laughed.

Logan grinned, he'd missed this, the banter from home and he turned to look at Tina, whose eyes were flying all around. "It's okay, this is normal joking with our lot," he whispered and her body relaxed before she gave a small smile.

"Clayr," Tina spoke quietly. "I can give you tips on who's who here and there's more Wolves that'll be joining us. My cousin, Nate, is on his way and he is a great guy, good looking, loyal, and a fabulous Wolf."

Logan snorted as Tina tried to hide a smirk at the same time as Mason scowled. "You're not helping, Tina." Mason looked as if he was going to burst a blood vessel as Clayr cocked her head to the side.

"There's a but, isn't there?" she asked, looking at Logan's face then at Tina.

"I didn't say there was a but." Tina tried hard to stop herself laughing, biting her bottom lip.

"I know you didn't." Clayr eyed her again. "I can sense there is though. So spill, what is it?"

Tina shrugged. "Oh, didn't I mention he's coming back with his mate, Brett?"

The entire table erupted in laughter as Clayr threw another piece of bread towards Tina. "So not funny!"

"Yes," Logan said with a grin, "it is."

The next hour was one Logan would keep locked inside his memories for a very long time. Several more of his countrymen joined them, with jokes, catch-up, and laughter filling the kitchen. Tina was as relaxed as he'd seen her, participating in the conversation and totally at ease, even if she stayed glued to his side.

He watched Ryder the entire time, gauging the youngster and his place within the Pack. "Ryder," he finally addressed the Panther. "If you're as good at tracking as you say, why don't you see if Mason can use you for hunting? Mason, what do you think?"

Ryder's face lit up, turning quickly to see what Mason would say. Clayr also turned to her brother. "Well?" she said cockily, smirking at him cheekily.

"I'll give him a try out." Mason nodded at Logan before facing Ryder. "You take orders from me, remember that, and you do not engage in a hunt unless I've given you permission. Your job is to locate and track, that's all. Understood?"

"Yes," Ryder beamed. "Anything you say, Mason." He turned to Logan. "Thank you."

"Don't thank me yet." Logan smiled. "You've not worked with him. Mason is a hard taskmaster so I hope you're up to the job."

"He is," Clayr stated firmly.

"I'll work hard and do my best," Ryder said solemnly. "I guess I should go and get some rest."

Mason agreed. "Aye, off ye go, laddie. I want you up and ready for dawn. You can meet us outside here, okay?"

"Yes, sir." Ryder stood, grinning from ear to ear.

"My name's Mason, no sir required."

"Yes, s. . . Mason. See you tomorrow."

With that Ryder rushed away, his eagerness clear for everyone to sense. "Thank you, Logan." Clayr's voice hitched. "Sorry, it's just he's opened up to me and I won't tattle about anything he's said, but he deserves some support, peace and a place to be safe."

"He's safe here." Mason's hand lowered over his sister's. "You know that, sis, but Logan has to vet everyone new. You know that too. We do the same in Scotland. I presume every Pack does it."

"I know." Clayr shrugged. "I just feel sad for what he's gone through, that's all. I'm happy you've both given him a chance to prove himself."

"I'll let you know how he gets on when we get back." Mason patted her shoulder. "And, just for you, I'll try and not be too hard on him. How's that?"

"You're the best!" Clayr jumped up, her arms around her brother's neck in a tight hug.

"Stop!" Mason groaned. "You're strangling me."

Logan laughed before pushing his chair back. "Okay, folks, we're leaving. Mason, can you text me tomorrow and let me know how it went? I don't think I'll be around, not for a couple of days anyway."

Loud whoops and raucous remarks filled the kitchen as he pulled Tina up. Her face was scarlet as they left, his friends still shouting behind them.

"You owe me," Tina whispered as they walked back towards their cabin.

"I know." Logan smirked brazenly. "And I intend to make payment, over and over again, my lassie. I hope you ate plenty 'cause I've a feeling we won't be out of the bedroom for a while!"

"Logan!" Tina exclaimed. "You are incorrigible!"

"Aye, that I am." Logan chuckled as he pushed the door open, pulling her inside quickly.

"Now, let's get back inside that bed and have some fun."

Tina giggled as he rushed them through the living room, straight to the bedroom. As he kicked the door shut behind him his eyes locked on hers. "My mate." His voice husky as he stroked her face.

"My mate." Tina mirrored his action, her hand on his cheek. "Take me to bed," she murmured softly.

"Aye," was all he replied.

*****

As the jet descended Chastity stretched then snuggled into Cam's arms. "I can't believe how time has flown past. I'm happy to be coming home, but I enjoyed myself in LA. I really liked helping Stracey, 'specially with the charity stuff."

Cam's arm tightened around her, holding her close. "I know, it's as if the days just disappeared but I'm glad you enjoyed my home. Or rather, our other home. Stracey told me you were very enthusiastic about a couple of the charities we're involved in, so, I was thinking of putting you in charge of dealing with them. If that's something you think you'd be interested in doing when we're in LA?"

"Yes," Chastity answered quickly. "I'd love that and it means I won't be bored while you're doing your other business stuff. Thank you, Cam. I really appreciate you having the confidence in me to let me do that. I'll work hard, I promise."

"I know you will, baby." Cam sighed, his body tensing as the jet touched down. "Now for my conversation with Fergie. Wish me luck, honey."

"Hey," Chastity looked up into his face. "It'll be fine, trust me, Alpha."

"Thanks." Cam leaned down, kissing her quickly then stood back up. "Let's get it over and done with. Can you get Mac and Rory up to the cabin? I'll want to speak to them once I've dealt with Fergie. Also, can you ask Mac to contact Logan and Mason and get them to organize a Pack meeting there? Give me an hour and then we'll head over there. Okay?"

"Sure." Chastity nodded, taking his offered hand and getting up. Her fingers entwined with his, gripping his hard. "It'll all work out. I know it will."

"I hope so." Cam stated as the jet came to a smooth stop.

He didn't wait on Marcus opening the door, Cam did it himself and was lowering the steps as his pilot joined them. "In a hurry?" Marcus asked, an eyebrow raised.

"Yes," Cam replied quietly. "Can you organize everything to be brought to the cabin, please?"

"Yes, boss, I'll do that as soon as I've done my checks."

"Thank you," Cam threw over his shoulder as he exited the jet, Chastity right behind him.

The first thing both of them saw was Fergie standing waiting for them. "He's keen," Chastity whispered as they walked towards him.

"I would be too if I were in his shoes," Cam admitted. "Best get this over with."

As soon as they were within talking distance, Fergie gave a tight smile. "Welcome back. Hope your trip went okay."

"Thanks and yes it did." Cam held out his hand, Fergie shaking it firmly. "Now, cousin, why don't we go to the office and have that talk."

"Sounds good to me," Fergie answered, his body so tense that they could see it in his very stance.

Chastity squeezed Cam's hand and gave him a smile as they made their way to the Alpha's cabin, both of them waving and shouting "hellos" to Pack members on their way. When they got inside Marie and Angel were waiting, both of them as tense as Fergie, giving tight smiles and quiet "welcome backs."

Cam let go of Chastity's hand. "Go get Mac and Rory," he reminded her and she nodded before leaving quickly.

~ Chapter 16 ~

Cam took a deep breath and led his cousin to the office, hoping Fergie would agree to his plans. As soon as they got inside, he poured himself a drink. "Want one?" he asked and Fergie shook his head, standing stiffly at the door.

"Come in, close the door and let's sit down so you can hear me out." Cam went over to one of the soft armchairs at the fireplace.

Fergie said nothing as he joined him and Cam could sense the unease within the Wolf. "Firstly, I want to say I absolutely do not want bad blood between us, Fergie. We're family and that's the last thing I want. Secondly, I have some plans and I'm hoping you're going to agree. I hope what I've come up with, or I should say what Chastity helped me to come up with, is acceptable to you and both Packs."

Fergie sat up straight, his hands clasped tightly in his lap. "Go on."

"Okay, this is what I have planned . . ."

More than half an hour later, they left the office and found everyone in the living room. Marie and Angel looking as if they were about to burst from the strain. Chastity raised an eyebrow and Cam inclined his head slightly as Mac and Rory looked uneasy. Cam stopped in front of the fireplace and Fergie stood at his side, neither of them giving

208

anything away.

"Okay, I know you've been waiting to find out what's going to happen now that Fergie is back on his feet," Cam started slowly, looking around everyone present. "Chastity put something to me and we've talked about it a lot, honing some details and plans, and this is what I've proposed."

Cam paused, Angel's hand flying to her mouth, Marie's eyes wide, Mac and Rory looking decidedly on edge. The only one that seemed at ease was his mate. Chastity sat curled up in one of the armchairs, a serene look on her face. Cam gave her a small smile before carrying on.

"You all know I never wanted to be Alpha, but the situation arose where I just had to take on the mantle. However, what I wasn't expecting was to actually enjoy it, in fact, I love being Alpha. But we have Fergie, whose birthright is to be Alpha of this Pack and I will not, cannot, deny him that right. So, first things first, Fergie will be taking over as Alpha here, effective immediately."

Angel squealed as Marie's face grew wet from tears streaming down her face. Cam held up his hands though because he was far from finished. "I'm not finished. I'm going to take on Chastity's old Pack, but Fergie and I have agreed to work together on several proposals I have planned. The two Packs are going to work as one on these projects and everyone will get more details about those soon."

Cam paused, his eyes settling on Rory and Mac. "I'll be renaming the Wild Flower Pack, but you two need to decide where you want to be. Fergie has said he would love for both of you to be a part of his Pack, but, my friends, I want you too. The decision is yours. If you need some time to think about it, that's fine. Just let either of us know when you've made up your mind."

Mac stepped forward. "I'm going with you, Cam. No offence, Fergie, but my loyalty lies with Cam."

Fergie inclined his head. "No offence taken, Mac, and I'm sorry to see you leave, but I wish you well in your new Pack."

Rory bit his bottom lip, looking at Cam and then Fergie. "Okay," Rory held his hands out then dropped them. "Cam, I've got to stay here, I'm sorry, but Charlie needs to be here right now. She's going to need the support of her friends and family . . ."

Cam interrupted. "Is there something wrong with her? Is she ill? I can get her to the best doctors, Rory, just say the word."

Rory gave a lopsided grin. "No, she's not ill. But, her *condition* means she wants to stay close to the Pack she grew up in. She's going to kill me for letting the cat out of the bag, but my mate is pregnant."

Cam's mouth dropped open as his eyes flashed to Chastity. His mate just smiled knowingly as Mac grabbed Rory in a bear hug. Cam went over, clapping him on the back. "That was the last thing I expected to hear but I'm pleased for you! For both of you and I understand why she'd want to stay here."

"Thanks, Cam, I'm glad you understand."

Fergie joined them. "This is fabulous news! We always celebrate when one of our women is pregnant so I'll need to organize something for you both."

Rory looked horrified. "No! Not yet. As I said, she's gonna kill me for telling you, she wanted to keep it under wraps for a little while longer."

"Aah, okay." Fergie grinned. "We can't have her getting upset so we won't do the Pack announcement just yet."

"Thank goodness." Rory laughed. "She's a little, now what's the word?" He tapped the side of his head. "Darn crazy! Aye, that's it, she's a little nuts at the moment, but she says it's to do with the hormones stampeding through her system."

"That's true," Marie agreed. "She-Wolves have a shorter pregnancy than humans, so our hormones explode for the first few weeks. Just leave her be and she'll be fine soon, Rory. Don't worry and I'll inform the healer so she can get ready for the birth. We use some locally grown herbs and plants to make a good remedy to help with labor and the pain, so she'll need to go and source it now to ensure she

211

has enough when the time comes."

"Okay, sounds like a plan." Rory seemed to relax. "But, Marie, please don't let Charlie know I've told you. She wants to do the announcement in a couple of weeks. She's very excited about it and I don't want to steal that from her."

"Oh, you don't need to worry, we women know how to keep secrets. Angel and I will not say a word, apart from speaking to the healer and she never gossips, but I'll make sure she knows to keep it to herself."

"Thanks. Now, if you'll excuse me, I have to go hunt down a rabbit." Rory shrugged. "She's got a hankering for rabbit stew and, apparently, we don't have any. Cam, I'll see you later on and I wish both of you well with the new situation."

Cam nodded, patting him on the back again as Fergie held up a hand to stop him. "Rory, I'd like you to continue with organizing security, but I'd also like to offer you the position of Beta. Would you be interested in that?"

Rory's smile lit up the room, his chest puffing out as he stood straight, staring at Fergie then lowering his eyes. "Yes, I'd be honored, thank you, Alpha."

"Good." Fergie waved him away. "Now go and get your mate some rabbit before she skins you and puts *you* in the pot. We can discuss things tomorrow, say ten, okay?"

"I'll be here." Rory grinned as he almost ran from the cabin.

"Thank you," Cam acknowledged the significance of Fergie making Rory his Beta. "He's a good Wolf, strong, loyal, and will fight to the death to protect his loved ones and the Pack."

"I know." Fergie nodded. "He's an asset and I'm glad he decided to stay. I also hope he stays after the baby is born."

Cam shrugged. "I can't say for sure, but making him Beta was a good move. If anything would keep him here it's that."

Fergie smirked. "That's what I'm betting on."

"I'm relieved we could sort this out, cousin," Cam admitted, holding his hand out to Fergie.

"Me too." Fergie ignored Cam's hand, grabbing hold of him in a hug, each patting the other's back.

"Right, Mac, go and get your things, we'll head over to Wild Flower soon, once we've packed our things from here."

Mac nodded, disappearing quickly as Chastity stood. "Marie, those wrapped up presents that Marcus brought, is it okay if I leave them here? They're for Charlie and Rory, once they announce the pregnancy then I'll give them what we brought."

Marie looked confused, frowning. "What? How did you know?"

Cam laughed. "Don't ask. It's some sort of gift she's got, but she wouldn't tell me who it was, only that someone was pregnant."

"Good gracious." Marie chuckled. "Yes, of course, I'll store them in one of the spare rooms. Cam, Angel and I will pack everything for you and we'll have it all taken over to Wild Flower. It's our job to do that for you. But, I'm wondering, where are you and Chastity going to stay? There's no Alpha cabin."

"We'll stay in one of the empty ones for the time being, but I've already got that under control. The men should've already started building our new cabin, I organized it while we were in LA. It'll take a few weeks to be ready, but it should be under way. I've also got a new vehicle being delivered. I think you'll like it, Fergie. I'll drop in and let you see it when I get the chance."

Fergie grinned. "Can't wait, I expect it'll be something a bit more upmarket than our usual jeeps."

"Aye, it is that." Cam smirked. "Oh, I meant to ask earlier, is it okay for my jet to continue to use your strip until I get one built over at my new Pack?"

"Of course," Fergie agreed.

"Good, thanks, Marcus will be leaving soon and he'll be back tomorrow morning with Rebecca and Jacob. The four of us have something we need to attend to but I'll come and pick them up. If you're around I'll show you my new toy."

"Fine, and if you need any help with getting the new landing strip done then all you need to do is ask."

Cam shook his head. "I think we'll be okay, we've got more Wolves arriving from Scotland and, from what I've heard, there are others that have returned home. Ones that left when Dupont arrived."

"Yes, I've heard that too." Fergie frowned. "I've also heard there are some others as well, Wolves that heard the Pack were looking for members."

"Don't worry, Fergie, I'll vet everyone before I allow them to stay permanently." Cam's face grew serious. "Jacob will be working his magic to find out all we can about any possible new arrivals."

"Good. We don't want any troublemakers."

"No, I'll ensure we don't have any." Cam held out his hand to Chastity. "Can we get a lift over?"

Angel stepped forward. "I'll take you, it's no trouble and I'll bring Mac over later, once he's packed."

"Thanks," Cam said as Fergie nodded his approval.

"Okay, honey, let's go break the news."

"Yes, Alpha." Chastity allowed him to lead her from the cabin where they'd first made love, where they truly *fell* in love, with a skip in her step and excitement humming through her body.

The drive was done in silence until they neared Wild Flower Camp when Angel spoke softly. "Thank you, Cam. I really appreciate what you've done and the way you handled things."

Cam sighed. "It was the only way to go without some kind of confrontation, Angel, and that was something I did not want. Fergie is very dear to me and I'm happy that he's healed."

"I know, and that just shows the kind of man and Wolf you are, Cameron Sinclair." Angel gave him a small smile as they came to a stop.

"I'll see you soon." Cam got out, helping Chastity down.

"Hope so." Angel grinned, did a three point turn, and drove away.

"Home." Chastity breathed, leaning into Cam's side.

"Yes. Now we need to talk to the Pack." They started walking and saw Logan with two unknown males, Tina's arms around the neck of one as she seemed to be squealing in delight. "Wonder who that is?"

As they drew nearer Logan spotted them. "Hi, nice to see you back."

"Hi to you too." Cam looked at the two men, one tall and dark with tattoos showing above his collar and on his arms, the other shorter with brown hair and a piercing in his eyebrow. Cam raised an eyebrow. "Why don't you introduce me?"

Tina jumped back, her face full of delight. "This is my cousin, Nate, and his mate, Brett. They've just returned home."

Cam held his hand out. "Nice to meet you."

Nate, the smaller Wolf stepped forward. "Glad to be home. It's been hard being away for so long but we're here and ready, willing, and able to help put the Pack back together again. Anything you need from us, just ask, Alpha."

Cam noted his use of the title, even though he hadn't been introduced as such. "Glad to hear it."

Brett gave a cocky grin. "Nice to meet you, Alpha. Now, I may be out of line here, but I need to ask before we unpack . . . is there a problem with us being here?"

Tina's hand flew to her mouth as she shrieked. "Brett!"

Brett turned to her. "Tina, honey, ya'll know I love ya and we love it here, always have, but ya know that not all Packs accept Nate and me being together. I'm not putting him through any more upset or heartache, so, we need to know where we stand."

Cam looked over the two men, sizing them up as he kept a stern face. "Brett, we've never had a problem with same sex matings. I wouldn't allow any discrimination like that in any Pack of mine. So, you two being together is not a problem. However, any and all newcomers will be vetted by me and by

217

my associate, Jacob. I won't allow anyone membership until I'm certain they'll be an asset to the Pack as a whole, and aren't here for any other reason than to help make this Pack flourish. I hope you understand that."

Brett lowered his eyes. "I do and those terms are acceptable. Nate and I will work hard to help the Pack in any way we can, Alpha."

"Good. I'm glad to hear that." Cam turned to Logan. "Has the Pack been told of the meeting?"

"Yes," Logan replied. "They'll all be outside the front of the Alpha's cabin in about fifteen minutes."

"That's great, gives me time to see how the building work is coming along." Cam strode off, stopping when Brett spoke.

"Building work? I can help with that, I studied architecture and I'm a trained building engineer. Do you have plans I can look at?"

Cam looked over the man again. He certainly didn't look like any architect he'd met before but if he truly was trained then he'd be invaluable to the Pack. "Yes, Logan has the plans I emailed him last week. You two can work together and any changes run by me first, okay?"

"Sure thing." Brett grinned. "I like nothing better than creating a nice building, cabin, store, I've built the lot."

Cam reassessed the Wolf. "Well, you're

going to be kept very busy. I have several projects that I'm starting here. One of which is going to be a kind of orphanage for runaway kids and also for youngsters of other species that a Pack doesn't want. We have a Panther boy here now, his own Pack didn't make his life easy so he left when he was still a cub. I won't allow that, they need somewhere to come and be safe."

Brett's eyes lit up as he turned to Nate. "That's where you come in, honey pie."

Nate stepped forward. "I've worked with human kids in shelters. I love kids and, well, with it being Brett and I, we won't have any of our own. So, Alpha, I'll be very happy if you'd let me help in that department."

Cam looked between the two men, inclining his head to study them for a moment. "Sounds as if you two will be just what we're looking for. So long as Jacob doesn't turn up anything, then I think we have a deal."

Tina rushed forward, her face bright and happy. "Thank you, Alpha."

It was then he saw it, marks on her throat, more than one, heading downward past her t-shirt. Cam's eyes turned to Logan, searching for, and finding, his marks. "Congratulations are in order are they not?" Cam asked as he pointed to Logan's bruises.

Tina blushed scarlet as Logan chuckled.

"Yes, Alpha, and we'd like to schedule our bonding ritual for whenever it suits. We're not in any rush as we've sealed our bond and we're living together, but whenever you can fit us in then that'll be great."

"Damn!" Cam cursed, Tina's face falling until he carried on. "I'll have to dance, again! Don't you know I'm getting too old for all that?"

Logan shrugged. "Hey, Alpha, it's tradition!"

"Aye, it is that." Cam grabbed Logan in a hug. "Congratulations, my friend, I'm happy for you."

"Thanks."

"Right, now come and show me how the cabin is coming and, Logan, did my new vehicle arrive?"

"Yes, it did. I'm jealous, Cam."

"You are *not* getting one." Cam scowled. "But I will let you drive it when I'm not here."

Logan whooped, punching the air with his fist as Cam carried on walking. "Men." Chastity laughed.

As they neared the Camp his eyes widened, his lips tugging up in a large smile. "So *this* was Mason's secret, was it?"

He looked all around, small clumps of wild Scottish Heather blooming all over. Chastity looked up at his face. "Yes, do you like?"

"I love it." Cam stopped, bending down on one knee to breathe in deeply. The scent from the

Heather invading his senses and whisking him back to the Highland, to his home.

"I'll need to thank him," Cam whispered, his fingers trailing over the familiar plant.

"He's got it all over, he said that it will thrive here and will take root and spread." Chastity sighed. "I hope so, it's beautiful."

"It will." Cam stood. "Come on, I've got something I want you to see."

~ Chapter 17 ~

Chastity was still grinning like an idiot when they stood in front of the assembled Pack. Her shock when she saw the brand new Range Rover sitting with the registration "WHITEY" had her speechless. Cam's laughter at her face was loud and long.

"I take it you like?" he asked as he opened the door to show her the interior.

"I love it!" she'd squealed.

"It's got leather interior and comes with every addition anyone could want. It's a lot comfier than the jeeps we've got here, but it's still got off-road capability and four wheel drive, which we need."

"Yes, it's got all the bells and whistles." Chastity laughed. "I look forward to playing with it when you give me the chance and I love the plate."

"I thought you might." Cam smirked.

Now Cam stood before the Pack, his eyes picking out a few strange faces and he made a note to meet them privately to gauge their suitability for entrance to the Pack. First he had to let them all know about the change in status.

"Thank you for coming." Cam raised his voice to address everyone. "I have news about the future of the Pack and the first thing I want to tell you is that I am your new Alpha."

Cam had to pause as clapping and cheers

rose all around him. When they quieted a little he raised his hands and carried on. "I have big plans for the Pack, plans that will help us grow and prosper, but also ones that will help our kind as a whole. We'll be working with Highland Wolf Clan Pack to build and manage a rescue center and orphanage for stray young Wolves who've had to leave their homes for whatever reason. We'll give them, and any young Shifter, a safe haven until they decide what they want to do. Whether that's stay with us, or possibly move on to another Pack, we'll do what's best for them. We'll also be building more luxury cabins on Highland land to cater for people with money . . . lots of money . . . to come and sample the wilderness. I have several other projects in mind but those are for the future. For the here and now we need to rebuild the Pack, rebuild the Alpha's cabin too, after all, I want my mate to have somewhere she can truly call home."

As Cam turned to smile at Chastity the Pack yelled loudly, agreeing that their white Wolf needed a home. Some adding that she needed the space for any cubs that may come along. Cam laughed as Chastity's face blushed a gorgeous shade of red as she scowled up at him.

"We need to move on, leave the past behind us and I have to advise you all that I plan on leading you as best as I can. I truly believe it was my destiny to come here. To find my mate and to lead this Pack as Alpha! I also want to tell you that there is going to be a change of name. I don't apologize for this. It is my choice, my decision as Alpha, but I hope you like the name I've decided upon."

Cam waited, watching to see their reaction. There were a few frowns but mostly the Pack looked on with anticipation. "The new name, and the one we will be known by from this day forward is, Wild Highland Heather Pack."

The reaction was immediate, clapping, shouting and nodding. "I have to admit, that wasn't the one I'd picked, but, on arriving and seeing Scottish Heather planted all around, well, the name just came to me. I hope the Pack flourishes as well as the Heather that Mason has so kindly planted."

Chastity moved closer, taking hold of his hand. "You changed it."

"Yes." Cam nodded. "As soon as I saw the Heather blooming I couldn't help myself. I hope you like it."

"Yes." Chastity reached up, kissing his cheek. "I love it, my Alpha," she whispered softly, her breath tickling his face.

"My Pack!" Cam shouted. "Let me introduce you to your She-Wolf Alpha! Chastity will take on the role as befits her position so bear that in mind if you have any problems. We'll both pour our hearts and souls into rebuilding this Pack. We'll make sure everyone is taken care of and we *will* make this Pack prosperous once again. So, Wild Highland Heather Pack, are you with us?"

The Pack howled their acceptance and Cam nodded calmly before roaring above the noise. "Then let's get to work!"

*****

As they arrived at the airstrip early the next morning, Chastity yawned and rubbed her eyes. "Tell me again, why in blazes we're up so early?"

"I want to get this over and done with and Jacob needs to get back to LA to get started on checking out the new Wolves." Cam opened his door and got out, but leaned back in to continue talking to his sleepy mate. "I won't feel truly comfortable with them until I know Jacob's made sure they're not hiding anything. So, we need to pick them up here, drive to the cabin, do what needs to be done, drive back here and they can fly back to LA. Long day but I promise I'll give you a nice massage this evening."

"Hmm, that sounds nice." Chastity yawned again as Fergie appeared, jogging over fully dressed and wide awake.

"Morning." He grinned, his eyes taking in the Range Rover. "Nice!"

"Thanks." Cam beamed like a kid.

"Too pricey for my pocket though." Fergie ran his hand along the roof.

225

"If things go as I hope then both of our Pack's will be better off. You might get one then." Cam wouldn't insult his cousin by offering to buy him one.

"Yeah, hope so." Fergie peeked inside. "Jeez, it's like the cockpit of a plane. How do you know what all those gizmos do?"

"Well, my dear cousin," Cam sighed theatrically. "There's this thing called a manual that comes with it! You know, *the driver's manual*! Amazing what information you can find in there."

Fergie punched his arm, hard. "And there's the old Cam I've been missing. Cocky and sarcastic as ever!"

Cam laughed, raising his eyes to the sky as he heard the jet approaching. "How was your first day as Alpha?" he asked Fergie.

"Good. No, great! I was born for it and although it felt a little weird to begin with, I kinda felt at home real soon."

"I'm glad." Cam gave him a sad look. "I'm just sorry about the reason for it. I'm sorry I couldn't save your father."

"Don't." Fergie held up a hand. "Don't ever think that. You saved the Pack, Cam, and I'll always be grateful. So, cousin, do you need my help today? I get the vibe that whatever you four are up to could be dangerous?"

Cam shook his head. "No, we'll be fine, plus

it'd be kinda dumb if both of us do go and something goes wrong. Then both Packs would be without an Alpha. I'm not expecting things to go badly today. Truth be told I think Rebecca is over-dramatizing things, but, and it's a big but, if anything does go wrong, will you look after my Pack until the new Alpha is elected?"

"Hmm, I guess you're right and of course I will." Fergie's hand landed on Cam's arm. "Be careful, Cam."

"I will." Cam placed his hand on top of Fergie's. "I've picked several Wolves to be Beta, because I'll be commuting a lot I need more than one. Jinx, obviously, with Mac and Mason are who I've chosen and Logan is in charge of security. So if anything does happen then the Alpha position should be between those."

"Okay." Fergie frowned again. "Cam, I'm feeling real uneasy about this trip you're going on. What is it and why is Rebecca worried?"

"I'll tell you all about it some other time. It's something we need to do and I'm sure Rebecca is worrying about nothing. Don't stress, I'll text you when we're on our way home."

"You better." Fergie turned to leave. "'Bye you two, gotta go do some work now."

Chastity managed a small wave as she yawned, again, as the jet came to a stop not far from them. "Can we pick up coffee on the way?" she asked Cam as Jacob and Rebecca walked towards them.

Jacob looked grim and Rebecca looked tired, strained, and dressed in jeans, jumper and biker boots, she looked far removed from her usual impeccable self. Cam waited until they reached them. "Morning, you both okay?"

Jacob growled as Rebecca snorted. "At this time in the morning? Okay is not a word I'd use, Cameron."

They got in the rear, Jacob not even commenting on the new car as Cam got in and drove off. "Morning," Chastity said, turning to give them a smile. "I've asked him to stop for coffee, lots of coffee."

Rebecca inclined her head. "Good idea."

Jacob stared straight ahead, his eyes cold and hard. They'd stopped at a local bakery, bought coffee and pastries, and were half way through them before he spoke. "You brought anything to help start the fire?" These were the first words he said, his tone detached and harsh.

"Yes," Cam answered. "Gallon of gas in the rear. Are you okay, Jacob?"

"Yes," the large PI replied.

"Okay, but you don't sound it, and you don't look it." Cam waited on the cutting response he knew would come.

"He's just pissed because I refused to allow

you two to go alone." Rebecca nibbled on her pastry. "He'll get over it."

A low growl from Jacob filled the interior. "I see. Well, big man, you just have to suck it up. They're coming and that's already been decided. No point in having a hissy fit now."

Jacob didn't respond, his eyes staring straight ahead. Chastity turned to look at him then Rebecca, shrugging as she turned back around. "I'm going to try for a nap. Wake me when we get there."

"Okay, honey." Cam patted her knee as she curled up in the large seat, closed her eyes and promptly fell asleep.

Cam carried on, driving in the awkward silence, trying to start a conversation several times before giving up. He stayed quiet until they neared their destination, gently shaking Chastity awake. "We're nearly there, baby."

Chastity yawned, stretched, and then smiled. "I feel much better."

"I'm glad." He smiled over at her as he turned down the track that led to the cabin.

Slowing down as the building came into view, he stopped and turned around. "You ready?"

Rebecca nodded as Jacob's jaw clenched. Cam opened his door. "Okay, let's get this over and done with."

Jacob helped Rebecca out, her bag held in her arms against her chest. Cam could feel her nerves and as they drew closer to the cabin he saw her shiver. At that same moment Chastity growled a warning, her lip curling as she snarled loudly. "What? What is it?" he asked, wondering what the hell was wrong.

Chastity looked at him wide eyed. "What do you mean? Can't you *feel* that?"

Jacob's arm wound around Rebecca's shoulders as Cam shook his head. "I've no idea what you're talking about."

"There's something wrong here. Very wrong," Chastity whispered, her eyes darting all around.

"Their spirits are still here." Rebecca's voice full of pain as she stepped forward. "Hold this." She held her bag out to Jacob who took it quickly.

Rebecca opened the bag, taking out a handful of candles, which she proceeded to place around the cabin. Cam watched as she disappeared around the corner, Jacob right beside her, and waited until she reappeared. Then she started again, talking quietly as she started to light the candles, again disappearing and reappearing a few minutes later.

Chastity ran her hands up and down her arms. "My hair's standing on end, with goosebumps, there's something wrong here, Cam."

"What happened inside that building was very wrong, baby."

When all the candles were lit Rebecca

withdrew what looked like a bunch of dried herbs, tied together with various colored twine. When she lit this she turned to Jacob. "We need to go inside. Bridget needs to leave. I feel her pain, Jacob, she's sorry and scared."

"No." Jacob shook his head. "I don't want you to go in there, Becca. It's not pretty. Fuck, it's a bloodbath in there. Please, honey, don't go in."

Rebecca shook her head, her eyes sad as she looked up at Jacob. "I have to, baby, I have to set her free."

"What about *him*? What if he's there?" Jacob whispered, his voice tortured and full of worry.

"He is." Rebecca nodded. "I can feel him. But it's Bridget that I need to help."

Cam cursed, kicking his foot in the dirt, stepping forward to stand next to the Witch. "She betrayed you, Rebecca, you don't owe her anything."

"I know I don't, Cam, but it's the right thing to do. If I don't she'll be trapped here, with *him* and I can't allow that."

Chastity growled again, her fangs descended as if she was going to shift. "Cam, whatever it is I can feel, it's getting stronger. I'm, fuck, Cam, I'm scared."

Cam moved quickly, pulling her into his arms. "It's okay, I won't let anything hurt you."

Chastity shivered in his arms as Rebecca

started to walk towards the broken door. She hummed as she walked, waving the smoking herbs before her as she went. When she reached the door she stopped, straightening her back then taking the final step inside. Jacob was beside her, his hand on her elbow as they entered the room where they'd found the decimated body of Bridget.

Cam looked at his mate. "Stay here, I have to go in case I can help."

Chastity shook her head. "I'm coming. You're not leaving me alone."

Cam couldn't argue, he didn't have time as he'd lost sight of Rebecca and Jacob. Holding Chastity's hand he strode quickly forward and into the cabin. Rebecca was standing with tears streaming down her face as she mumbled words that held no meaning to him. Jacob's face chalk white as he clenched his teeth hard.

"Bridget, you have to leave, you have to pass through. If you don't do it now you'll be stuck here, with him, and I won't be able to help you. Please, I know you're sorry, I can feel you, please, please, pass through."

Chastity gasped a mere moment before the walls shook, a loud shriek of anger almost deafening them. "Nooooooo! Never!"

Cam's blood ran cold as he looked around them trying to figure out what he could attack to help keep them safe. But, there was nothing, well nothing solid.

The walls continued to shake as a chair lifted from the floor and flew towards Rebecca. Jacob saw it and jumped in front of his mate, taking the full force of the flying object on his outstretched arms. Rebecca flinched, stepping towards him but he shook his head. "No, Becca, carry on, do what ya gotta do and do it fast so I can burn this fucker to the ground."

Rebecca's face hardened as she nodded, her voice rising in a prayer to the Goddess to help her child to pass into her arms. Chastity looked all around, her eyes wide and scared as various pieces of furniture were raised and sent flying all around. Cam held her close and almost fell to his knees as a table took him by surprise and hit him hard on his shoulders.

Jacob stood guard around Rebecca, batting things away when they came too close, or taking the full brunt of things too large for him to throw out of the way. Rebecca's voice seemed to dim but Cam realized it was the sounds in the room that made it seem that way. Loud screams and shrieks filled their ears as well as the sound of the breaking furniture.

Chastity's face was white as a sheet and he tried to usher her towards the door. She shook her head, clinging to him tightly as Rebecca carried on. After what seemed like hours, but was most probably only minutes, Rebecca raised her arms above her head, screaming words with a volume he'd never before heard.

Her entire body vibrated, power emanating from within, as another sound echoed around them. Soft crying, hiccups, and the word "sorry" reverberated around the room as Rebecca continued to perform whatever rite she was roaring. Cam tried to keep his eyes on her and he saw the moment her arms dropped, her knees giving way as Jacob grabbed her quickly, picking her up to cradle her in his arms.

"We're out of here," Jacob bellowed and Cam pulled Chastity with him, getting out as quickly as he could while objects still assaulted them from all directions.

When they crossed the doorway the noise abated, but only slightly, as Cam ran towards the Range Rover to get the accelerant to burn the cabin to the ground. Rebecca lay limply in Jacob's arms as Cam ran frantically around the cabin, spilling gas as he went before throwing the container in the doorway.

He picked up one of the lit candles, holding it out to Jacob who fumbled to hold Rebecca with one arm. Jacob took the candle and dropped it on the gas, shouting as the flame ignited and swiftly a ring of fire burned around the cabin before the flames erupted within. "Burn in hell you bastard!"

The bloodcurdling screams from within

caused Cam to shiver, reaching for Chastity he held her close as they stood watching the place burn to the ground. Cam was surprised at the ferocity of the fire, wondering if Rebecca's magic had anything to do with it. But he still worried about the flames spreading and affecting the trees dotted all around.

He looked around and spotted what he hunted for, an outside tap and hose. He waited until the cabin smoldered before them then turned the water on, hosing down both the ruined remains of the cabin and the surrounding area. Cam walked around and around, making sure there were no stray sparks that could cause a problem, even though the ground was damp and the possibility slight.

When he was satisfied everything was safe, he returned to find Rebecca still in Jacob's arms as his friend stared at the remnants of the place that had seen such horror. Chastity was sitting in the front seat of the Rover, her face white, as she sipped on some bottled water.

Cam walked over and gently placed a hand on Jacob's shoulder. "It's over, come on, let's get you home. Is Rebecca going to be okay or do we need to stop off somewhere? Like a hospital?"

Jacob shook his head. "She'll be fine. She woke to say she was exhausted but she needed to rest."

"Okay." Cam nodded. "That's good. Come on, Jacob, let's leave this place behind forever. It's over, my friend."

"Is it?" Jacob asked, his eyes full of pain. "He didn't pass over. We all know that. Does that mean he can find us? Attack us? I'm not sure it is over, Cam."

"I've no idea." Cam shook his head. "I didn't even believe in ghosts until earlier so I can't answer. But it's over for today, we need to leave and get Rebecca back. You need to take her home, Jacob."

"Yes," Jacob agreed, taking one last look at the charred remains before striding to the car.

~ Chapter 18 ~

"I'm looking forward to this, and the rest!
The past couple of weeks have been manic."
Chastity plopped back down beside Cam on the sofa
as they flew back to LA.

"I know." Cam sipped the drink she'd just
given him, savoring the burn as it slid down his
throat. "My muscles are aching. Another bonding
ceremony, another dance, I hope there's no more for
a while. My body can't take it."

"Oh, I don't know 'bout that, Alpha."
Chastity poked him in the ribs. "You were full of
energy that night if I remember right!"

"That, my dear, was pure adrenaline." Cam
chuckled, moving his glass to his other hand and
putting his arm around her. "And Rory and Charlie's
news is out. Did you see Logan striding around
yesterday? You'd think it was him that was going to
be a father, not his brother."

"They're twins, Cam. They're closer than
most brothers. He looked so happy, telling everyone
that would listen that he was going to be an uncle.
That this would be the first Highlander baby. It was
so cute."

Cam almost choked on his drink. "Cute?
Damn, don't let him hear you say that."

"Well, it was." Chastity tucked her legs
underneath her, getting comfy. "Charlie was

overjoyed with her presents. She said to thank you, I think her words were along the lines of 'Tell Cam thank you a million times!' and I'm so pleased for Logan and Tina. I was worried about her, real worried. I wasn't sure she'd come back from the dark place she was in. But looks as if Logan did it. I'm sure it was him that healed her."

"Yes, the difference in her is quite remarkable, but I think having her cousin around has helped too."

"I love those two!" Chastity gushed. "Nate is adorable and Brett, well, damn but he is going to be so much help to the Pack. He's got some amazing ideas."

"He does and yes I'm happy they've rejoined the Pack." Cam looked thoughtful for a moment. "I'm thinking of putting Nate in charge of the orphanage, what do you think?"

Chastity didn't answer straight away, she thought on her reply then nodded. "I think that's a good fit. He's really good with the little ones and he's got the patience of a saint. Plus, the way he looks I think that youngsters will relate, you know? Yes, I think that's a splendid idea."

"Okay, I'll tell him when we get back."

"Things are coming together, Cam." Chastity beamed. "The Pack is growing stronger by the day, with the new Highlanders, and the other Wolves that have come asking to join the Pack. Plus, our cabin is coming along nicely, I can't wait for it to be finished, but Brett said it's another month away, at least."

Cam kept his face deadpan, hiding his secret well. "Yes, I know, baby, but it won't be too long. A month will fly past."

"I guess," she murmured then sat up, her face animated. "Cam, this handfasting ceremony we're going to, is there anything I should be doing, not doing, taking, not taking? I've no idea about it and I don't want to do something wrong or upset Rebecca."

"I've already asked her and she said just to come as if you were going to any other bonding ceremony, or marriage, but she did say to wear shoes that are easy to take off. Apparently we'll be barefoot for the actual ceremony."

"Barefoot's okay. I'll just wear a simple dress with sandals. What about a present?"

Cam grinned. "Already taken care of. I'm giving them a honeymoon in the Bahamas. Both of them love the sea and there's some of the most wonderful beaches there."

"They'll love that." Chastity snuggled closer.

"It's not long until we go to Vegas so what about you getting your gown this trip?" Cam still couldn't believe his mate wanted to be married in Sin City.

"Good idea. I'll go with Stracey and see if I can find something."

"Okay, remember, Chastity, you get anything you want and do not think about the price of anything."

"I'll try." She giggled as he tickled her side.

"I mean it. Anything you want."

"Okay!" She relented so he'd stop her torture.

"Right, we have a busy schedule these two weeks. We've got the handfasting tomorrow, then I've got business meetings backed up for the next few days. Stracey has organized for you to meet those two charities you're interested in to see about becoming a hands-on sponsor. So we'll both be busy. We probably won't see a lot of each other during the day but I promise I'll be finished work by early evening."

"I'll do the same." Chastity nodded, her eyes wide. "Who would've thought I'd be doing all this charity work? I'm excited and a little scared at the same time."

"Don't be." Cam reassured her. "You'll be great. Just remember, if anyone acts like a jackass, bring out your Alpha Wolf, they'll soon back down, honey."

"Good advice. I'll try and remember that."

"We'll be landing soon, Jinx is picking us up and dinner will be ready when we get there. I think we should have an early night, baby, what with us having a hectic schedule 'n all."

Chastity looked up, frowning. "Hmm, is that the real reason, Sin, or is it because you're horny?"

Cam forced a shocked look onto his face. "What? I'm wounded, Chastity. I'm just thinking of you, honey, so you can get enough rest."

"Yeah, right." She laughed. "I think an early night sounds good, but, I want champagne and strawberries, along with a nice hot water filled Jacuzzi!"

"Oh, I think I can arrange that, my mate." Cam leaned down, kissing her soft sweet lips.

*****

"Are you sure I look okay?" Chastity asked for about the hundredth time as they pulled into Jacob's drive.

"The answer is yes, the same as it was the other hundred times you asked." Cam chuckled. "Relax. It's just us four and some of her coven."

"Relax he says." Chastity turned around to face Stracey. "Have you met these Witches? Do you know them?"

Stracey leaned forward, patting Chastity's shoulder. "Will you calm down? Everyone here is here to celebrate their ceremony. So, deep breath and smile."

"I can't relax." Chastity squirmed in her seat. "I know you, and Rebecca, but well, any other magical peeps I've met weren't so nice, and that's putting it mildly."

"Trust me. Everyone here is nice, well mostly." Stracey smiled with an evil glint her eye.

Jinx pulled her to him. "Will you stop it? You're scaring her."

"See." Chastity poked Cam. "Did you hear that? Mostly. She said mostly."

Cam glowered over his shoulder at Stracey. "I told you she was nervous but, oh no, instead of reassuring her, you scare her. Good going."

"What?" Stracey looked all wide eyed innocence. "She's a freaking Alpha She-Wolf and she's scared of a few Witches? Sorry, Chastity, I was only joking, honestly."

Chastity still squirmed in her seat causing Cam to sigh. "Enough already. Chastity you look fabulous and everyone here is here for one thing only and that's to celebrate Rebecca and Jacob's handfasting ceremony."

He pulled the car to a stop, turned off the engine and turned to his mate. "Relax, baby."

"I'll try." She smiled, taking a few deep breaths.

Cam came around helping her out of the car and led her to the door which lay open. As they went inside she gasped as they took in the beautiful interior. There were no lights on, the only illumination coming from a myriad of candles set around the entire area. Their eyes fell on Jacob's Japanese Garden that was transformed with white gossamer falling over the greenery, white petals floating on top of his pond where his fish swam lazily beneath. A wooden altar stood next to the pond and Elijah gave them a wave. "Hi." The High Priest welcomed them.

"If you come and join us, but first I ask that you remove your shoes. I've already blessed the circle and made it pure for the ceremony."

They slipped off their shoes and went over to join the dozen or so other people who stood around, all smiling brightly. Chastity held Cam's arm tightly as they took their places. "Do we need to do anything?" Chastity whispered.

She jumped when a hand touched her arm, a middle aged woman shaking her head. "No, dear, we're just here to witness their binding to each other."

"Oh, okay. Thanks." Chastity gave the woman a smile.

"You're welcome, any friends of Rebecca's are friends of ours. Blessed be."

Chastity just stared, not knowing how to respond. Cam stepped forward. "Thank you. We're not familiar with the ceremony and don't want to offend anyone."

"Oh, you wouldn't do that." The woman chuckled. "We're used to people who aren't of our faith joining in on the handfasting ceremonies. Truth be told there should be a High Priestess doing the ceremony but Rebecca has broken with tradition saying she wanted Elijah only to perform it. He's quite excited about it all."

They turned to look at Elijah, looking rather somber in a black cloak with a hood, which covered him from head to foot. The rest of the coven dressed in a variety of different styles, from velvet, long dresses with lace up corsets, to long white cotton gowns, and also some dressed in the same type of cloak, in varying colors, as that which Elijah wore.

Chastity squirmed again and Cam pressed her hand with his. "Relax."

Elijah held up his hands and they all quietened down waiting on the ceremony to start.

"Let us first welcome the happy couple, Rebecca and Jacob. Blessed be."

The coven all whispered, "Blessed be" and then Jacob led Rebecca down the hallway. He was dressed in a plain black shirt and dress trousers and the smile on his face was huge. He nodded to everyone as Rebecca glided beside him.

She was a vision in a dark red velvet cloak that covered her entirely. The velvet was embroidered along its edges by white thread, with symbols and markings that they couldn't even begin to understand. Rebecca's head was bowed as Jacob led her to stand in front of the small altar.

Elijah lit a match, dropping it into an earthenware bowl atop the altar and a glorious scent filled the air. He raised his head, smiling as his hands rose high above him. "Friends, we are here today to see Jacob and Rebecca join hands and be bound together by their love, now and forever." Elijah smiled at Rebecca. "I have already cast the circle and consecrated this place. The circle is an infinite thing, magical, never-ending, it never changes and yet is always flexible. A ring with no beginning and no end."

Elijah picked up a bunch of dried herbs, lit it and started to wave it around Rebecca and Jacob. "Like the circle, true love is infinite. It goes on, knows no limits or constraints. It flourishes and blooms in the light, and in the dark, laying down no burdens, no ultimatums. Love in its infinite form is something that cannot be coerced, it cannot be taken away. It is a glorious gift we give to ourselves, and an honor we give to others, from the bottom of our hearts, bodies and souls."

Chastity sniffled and Cam handed her a tissue from his jacket pocket.

"When two people come together and give one another this marvelous gift, this most sacred gift of all, it is certain the universe is smiling down upon us, showering us with every blessing in its power. Today is a day to celebrate the love between Jacob and Rebecca. They are two people who are two halves of a whole. Two souls coming together to form one single being; their hearts beating in a single rhythm within this great universe. They are together as one, and so they will now light a candle of unity, to show the universe, the Goddess and us, that they are one light burning brightly within the darkness."

Elijah produced a small candle, placing it within the bowl on the altar. Rebecca and Jacob stepping forward, both striking a match and lit it together.

Elijah carried on. "Today we ask that the infinite light of the divine shine upon this union. So, in that spirit I offer a blessing to this ceremony. Blessed be this marriage with the gifts from the east – new beginnings that come each day with the rising sun, communication of the heart, mind, body and soul."

Elijah paused for a brief moment as the coven spoke as one. "Blessed be."

As Elijah continued Cam was distracted by Chastity's arm slipping through his, her hand squeezing. Looking down at her she smiled up at him, mouthing silently, "I love you."

Cam smiled back, his eyes on hers as he mouthed back. "I love you too." When he turned back and tuned into the ceremony he realized he'd missed . . . well, he had no idea, only knowing he'd definitely missed something.

Elijah was shaking the smoking herbs to four

corners before looking forward once again. "Rebecca, Jacob, these four simple blessings will aid you on your life journey that begins today. However, they are but tools. These tools are what you must use together to create the light, the strength, and the infinite energy, now and forever, of a love you so richly deserve."

The High Priest smiled at the couple, raising an eyebrow and looking them both in the eye before carrying on. "Now, I bid you look into one another's eyes, hearts and souls. Jacob, please place the ring on Rebecca's finger and say your vows."

Elijah held out a simple plain band ring and Jacob picked it up to place it on Rebecca's finger, grinning down into her face. "I promise to love you, take care of you, and protect you with my dying breath. I promise, my love, that I'll make you happy, make you smile, and keep you content, each and every day. But, most of all I promise to cherish you above all others, hold you close and keep the darkness at bay. Quite simply, Rebecca, I'll adore you from now until eternity."

Rebecca's eyes glassed over and Cam was certain she had tears in her eyes as Jacob smiled down at her lovingly. He saw her take a few steadying breaths as Elijah turned to her. "Rebecca, please give Jacob the ring and state your vows."

Rebecca cocked her head to the side, waiting a moment before she whispered, "My Wolf, I promise to love you, cherish you, and look after you, from this day onward. I'll protect from harm, I'll stand by your side no matter what with joy in my heart. I'll hold your hand to lead you to the light so we both may bask in the Goddess' glorious blessing. I, my big bad Wolf, will be beside you from now 'til eternity." Rebecca grinned, a cheeky twinkle in her eyes as she placed the gold band on his finger. "Hope you're ready for a rocky ride," she quipped as the ring slid into place.

Jacob chuckled. "Anytime, Becca, for eternity, my love."

Elijah obviously only just managed to suppress his laughter, took a breath and carried on. "The vows of love have been declared. I ask you now to cross your hands over the other's, and take one another's hands."

Cam was entranced with the beauty of the ceremony as Rebecca and Jacob crossed their hands, his huge one covering her much smaller, delicate hand.

Elijah retrieved a woven twine cord from a pocket in his cloak. The cord made up of a myriad of colors with small knots set along its length. He gently bound their hands together and looked up into their faces. "Jacob, Rebecca, this cord symbolizes so much. It is your life, your love, and your bound hearts. It shows an eternal connection that the two of you have found with one another. The ties of this handfasting are not formed by this cord, or even the knots connecting them. They are formed instead by your vows, by your pledge, your souls, and your two hearts, now bound together as one. As one last bond, Jacob, will you please kiss Rebecca."

Rebecca smiled as Jacob's free hand snaked around the back of her head, holding her in place as his lips covered hers in a scorching kiss that lasted far longer than it should. They only broke apart when Elijah coughed and then the High Priest removed the cord. "Friends, it gives me great pleasure to present, Jacob and Rebecca, joined together for eternity."

Everyone started clapping as the couple turned around, Rebecca's smile huge as she undid the cord around her neck holding her cloak in place. Quickly slipping the red velvet from her to let it fall to the ground, revealing an ivory evening gown of satin and chiffon, a cowl neck at the front and backless, so low it skimmed the very top of her ass. "Now, where are my Manolo's?" She laughed, looking behind the altar and pulling a pair of stunning sandals out and placing her feet inside them.

"That's better! Now, folks, outside for food, drink and music, courtesy of Cameron!"

Cam stepped forward, pulling Rebecca into his arms and kissing her cheek. "Congratulations, honey, I'm so happy for both of you."

As he turned to congratulate Jacob, his friend

held out his hand. "I can't even put into words how happy I am, Cam, and thanks for the catering. It took a lot of pressure off Becca."

Cam shook his hand and shrugged. "My pleasure and I hope you enjoy your trip."

"We will." Jacob laughed and Cam moved away as the next person waited to congratulate the happy couple.

"Can I put my sandals back on now?" Chastity whispered when she caught up to him.

"Yes." Cam laughed, going in search of his own footwear.

Everyone started to make their way outside but Cam held off, wanting to check that Rebecca had fully recovered from their ordeal when they'd burned down the cabin. Soon it was just the three of them and he waited as Jacob leaned down, kissing her cheek and whispering. "I'll be out in a little bit."

Rebecca's hand trailed down his arm, squeezing his hand and nodding. "Okay, big guy, don't be long we don't want to keep our guests waiting."

As Jacob walked back down the hallway Cam took hold of her hand. "I just wanted to make sure you're alright. That you've recovered okay from our little trip?"

"Yes." She nodded, her eyes sad for a brief moment. "I was just tired and needed to rest for a day or so but I'm fine, honestly."

Cam smiled. "I'm glad. I was worried about you, Rebecca."

"No need." Rebecca's head lifted haughtily. "Ya know, I'm a tough cookie, Cam. Takes more than a ghost or two to take me down."

"Yes, I know, but doesn't stop me worrying about you."

She stepped forward hugging him hard. "Thank you, you know I love you, don't you?"

Cam hugged her back. "As I do you. Now, where's all this food and drink?"

Laughing she pointed through the doors and out where the pool was. "There. Go, eat and enjoy, I'll be out as soon as my Wolf appears back."

Cam kissed her cheek and went in search of Chastity. He found her chatting with Elijah, her hands moving around animatedly as she bombarded him with questions. Cam picked a drink from the tray of a passing waiter and joined them. "The service was lovely," he said to Elijah as soon as Chastity stopped to take a breath.

"Thank you." Elijah beamed. "It was such an honor as it's usually the High Priestess that performs these ceremonies."

"Well, for what it's worth, I think you did it perfectly." Cam shrugged. "But then again I've never been to any others." He laughed as Chastity pinched his arm, Elijah obviously seeing his humor and laughing too.

"Yes, well, it's something I'll treasure for a long time and I'm so ecstatic that everything's turned out so well." Elijah lowered his voice. "All that business with Bridget and Tobias was awful. It shook our coven to its core but Rebecca has assured everyone that things are going to be just fine."

"She's good at that," Cam said, turning to see Rebecca being kissed passionately by Jacob inside.

"Yes, she is." Elijah agreed. "Now, if you'll excuse me, I have to go mingle."

Chastity frowned. "Darn, I wanted to know more."

Cam laughed, pulling her into his side. "Honey, if you want to know more you can ask Stracey, or Rebecca, though I'd wait until Rebecca's back from her honeymoon."

"Good thinking." Chastity giggled. "Oh, Cam, can you believe this?"

Cam looked down at her, not quite getting what she meant. She smiled up at him and went on. "I mean, you and me, Stracey and Jinx, Rebecca and Jacob, and that's not even including Grant and Shelly, Rory, Charlie, Fergie being healed. So much has happened and sometimes I'm worried it's all a dream. That I'll wake up and I'll be back . . ."

Cam's finger shot up to cover her lips. "Shh, don't ever think that. This, all of this," Cam's hand waved around. "It's all real. *We* are real. It's only the beginning, Chastity. We have our whole lives ahead of us and from what we've got planned it's going to be a busy time, both here in LA and back at the Pack. So, my love, take tonight to simply enjoy, because come tomorrow we will be busy, busy, busy."

Chastity stretched up, kissing his cheek softly. "I adore you, Cameron Sinclair."

"I adore you too, my white Wolf." Cam's look full of love as he stared down into her starlit eyes.

*****

Jacob stripped quickly, opening his wardrobe and going inside. He picked out what he wanted and dressed as fast as he could, checking himself in the mirror several times before he took a deep breath and walked back down the hallway.

Rebecca stood at the end, waiting on him, and he fought not to laugh as her eyes widened and looked him up and down. She was talking before he even reached her. "What's this?" she said, her hand waving up and down his body.

He straightened his dark grey silk tie then tugged his suit jacket cuffs, a lighter grey than the tie he wore with a crisp white shirt. His dress trousers fitted like a second skin and he knew she could see his thick, muscular thighs clearly. He raised an eyebrow as his lips twitched up at the sides.

"This?" he queried as he stared down into her

eyes. "Don't you remember what I said to you when I caught you reading *that* book?" Rebecca's breath caught in her throat as she nodded. "Well, tonight, my ravishing Witch, I'm just reminding you that I'm far better than Mr. Grey, and I plan on showing you just how much better later tonight."

Rebecca's own eyebrow rose, a challenge in her eyes. "Are you now?"

Jacob lifted a finger, beckoning her forward. She took a step towards him and he pulled her into his embrace. His lips fell to hers and he kissed her with an abandon that really should've been kept for the bedroom. One hand in her glorious red hair and another on her skin where her dress barely covered her sweet ass. He heard her heart rate increase, her blood pumping through her system like a tsunami as he thoroughly ravaged her mouth.

As she melted into him he pulled back, a glint in his eyes. "You're mine, Becca, and tonight you're going to have the best night of your life."

"That's a bold statement, Wolf," Rebecca teased. "I've had several nights that I thought were my best."

Jacob chuckled. "Tonight will surpass anything you could've dreamed off. Tonight, my sassy Witch, I'll devour you, worship you, and have you roaring my name so loud the very Goddess herself will hear you."

Rebecca's eyes twinkled. "Now *that* is

something I look forward to, my big, and very bad, Wolf."

Jacob's stare was intense as he gazed down into her green eyes. "I'm so in love with you it hurts."

"Ditto, big guy, ditto." Rebecca took a deep breath. "We better go and see to our guests."

"Do we have to?" Jacob teased as she tugged his hand.

"Yes." She looked over her shoulder. "But it's going to be difficult to focus. After all, my mind is now on what you have planned for later."

"Good." Jacob smirked. "I want you to think of the pleasure I'm going to lavish on you, Becca."

"Oh, I will, Wolf, I will." As her laughter filled his ears, he let her lead him outside. His head and heart filled with pure joy and happiness.

"This is the most perfect day of my life," he whispered.

Rebecca tilted her head. "Yes, it is absolutely perfect, my Wolf."

They held each other's hand tightly as they walked out into the evening to join their friends to celebrate, both with smiles of joy lighting up their faces as they started their new life together.

Author's Note

Thank you so much for reading book 4 in the Highland Wolf Clan series. I sincerely hope you enjoyed it and you can read about Grant and Shelly's return to the Highlands in book 5! If you enjoyed this story then I would really appreciate if you could take a moment of your time to leave a review.

I'd like to say a huge *Thank You* to the girls on my Street Team. As usual, they've been so supportive and work so darn hard. You are totally awesome girls! Also the fabulous Missy Borucki my wonderful Editor, who it's a dream to work with. Thank you, Missy! Huge thanks to my Sassy Queens of Design, aka Becca, Angel and Stracey, for designing my covers and swag. I think this series' covers are my favorites!

Have a look for my other books, info over the page and come and join me for a chat on Facebook, and sign up for my mailing list, to get information on new releases.

Have a fabulous day and Live, Love, Read!

Ava xx

A K Michaels

Ava's Recommendations!

Want to read about the author I mentioned in the book? She's a real person and one of my most favorite human beings – Monica La Porta! Her stories are wonderful folks, so go and check her out.

I've loved all her books but my favorites are definitely the Immortal Series! Wonderful reads! So go and check her out on Amazon and if you stalk her on Facebook, then tell her you read about her in one of my books, lol.

Other Work by Ava

The Witch, The Wolf and The Vampire Series

Peri has been running since she was fifteen – using her magic to stay safe. 'They' can track her magic tho, so she has to use it sparingly. In Vegas, for a cash in hand job, and things turn nasty! She knows the amount of magic she would have to use to escape unscathed would bring 'them' right to her.

Before she can use the vast magic required two males appear and aid her. One a wolf, one an ancient vampire. Josef, the vampire, and Gabe, the wolf, are more than a little interested in this skinny girl. What ensues shocks both of the strong males – this girl is more than a stray, more than a witch – it looks like she is a mate – for both of them!?

Will Peri stay? Will they keep her safe? Who, if any, of the two will she choose? Just how much power does this stripling of a girl have locked inside her?

Adult content in this book!

Supernatural Enforcement Bureau Series

As Director of the Supernatural Enforcement Bureau, powerful Vampire Ronan, thought he had seen it all...until he discovers that Dragons actually exist. Can he help the Dragon being hunted on his patch? He certainly has the means at his disposal...if they can find it first...before the dark magic-wielding Witches and their Vampire cohorts.

After seeing the magnificent beast with his own eyes he can't turn from the task, even if he wanted to. Especially as his Sire, Josef, gives him a direct command to find the Dragon and keep it safe. No matter the cost.

With rogue Vampires and Witches on its trail, it's only a matter of time before they capture it. That's not something Ronan will allow...not on his watch! He will do whatever it takes to find and save the Dragon, using every powerful being at his disposal, including the dark and dangerous Creed.

Sabrina's Vampire Series

Sabrina's life was a mess, suspended from her police job, she ran to Vegas for a break, to escape the torment and embarrassment. She followed this up by getting blind drunk and down an alleyway with two thugs who wanted more than a goodnight kiss!

Kyle, a Vampire, hears her scream and against his better judgement enters the alley and saves her. As she collapses into his arms he had a deep need to take her home? He never takes anyone to his home! Soon Sabrina is ingrained in him - he can't get enough - can't let her go and just why are his bites not healing on her neck? When he finds out he is shocked - he must keep her - make her stay!

Will she? Will this woman stay in the arms of a Vampire?!

Defender's Blood Series

Alex has no idea her life is about to change beyond her wildest imaginings. She is the last in a long line of very special females born for a dangerous task, and she isn't sure she is up to it. Zach, her vampire protector, is just as sure she is.

Demon attacks, angels and even the ultimate, divine intervention, shake Alex to her very core. Can she do this? Can Zach keep her safe? The alternative is unthinkable: demons once more ruling the earth.

Zach has to ensure that Alex puts a stop to this - and quickly!

Read Defender's Blood, Alex's Destiny – Book 1 in the Defender's series.

Lori's Wolf

Lori's lost in the forest, regretting her idea to go for a hike. Hurt and getting more and more scared – especially when she hears the howls or a large animal nearby! In her haste to get away she falls and knocks herself out.

The large animal finds her, having heard her

screams!

The wolf changes and the Alpha looks down at the female. As soon as he picks her up his body reacts and he, at first, has no idea why! All he knows is his wolf wants out, wants to mark this human as his!

Lori is oblivious to what's in store over the next few days as the powerful Alpha carries her to his cabin!

Adult content in this novella.

12253069R00150

Printed in Great Britain
by Amazon.co.uk, Ltd.,
Marston Gate.